Donald MacKenzie and The Murder Room

>>> This title is part of The Murder Room, our series dedicated to making available out-of-print or hard-to-find titles by classic crime writers.

Crime fiction has always held up a mirror to society. The Victorians were fascinated by sensational murder and the emerging science of detection; now we are obsessed with the forensic detail of violent death. And no other genre has so captivated and enthralled readers.

Vast troves of classic crime writing have for a long time been unavailable to all but the most dedicated frequenters of second-hand bookshops. The advent of digital publishing means that we are now able to bring you the backlists of a huge range of titles by classic and contemporary crime writers, some of which have been out of print for decades.

From the genteel amateur private eyes of the Golden Age and the femmes fatales of pulp fiction, to the morally ambiguous hard-boiled detectives of mid twentieth-century America and their descendants who walk our twenty-first century streets, The Murder Room has it all. **>>>**

The Murder Room
Where Criminal Minds Meet

themurderroom.com

Donald MacKenzie 1908–1994

Donald MacKenzie was born in Ontario, Canada, and educated in England, Canada and Switzerland. For twenty-five years MacKenzie lived by crime in many countries. 'I went to jail,' he wrote, 'if not with depressing regularity, too often for my liking.' His last sentences were five years in the United States and three years in England, running consecutively. He began writing and selling stories when in American jail. 'I try to do exactly as I like as often as possible and I don't think I'm either psychopathic, a wayward boy, a problem of our time, a charming rogue. Or ever was.'

He had a wife, Estrela, and a daughter, and they divided their time between England, Portugal, Spain and Austria.

Henry Chalice

Salute from a Dead Man
Death Is a Friend
Sleep Is for the Rich

John Raven

Zalenski's Percentage
Raven in Flight
Raven and the Kamikaze
Raven and the Ratcatcher
Raven After Dark
Raven Settles a Score
Raven and the Paperhangers

Raven's Revenge
Raven's Longest Night
Raven's Shadow
Nobody Here By That Name
A Savage State of Grace
By Any Illegal Means
The Eyes of the Goat
The Sixth Deadly Sin
Loose Cannon

Standalone novels

Nowhere to Go
The Juryman
The Scent of Danger
Dangerous Silence
Knife Edge
The Genial Stranger
Double Exposure
The Lonely Side of the River
Cool Sleeps Balaban
Dead Straight
Three Minus Two
Night Boat from Puerto Vedra
The Kyle Contract
Postscript to a Dead Letter
The Spreewald Collection
Deep, Dark and Dead
Last of the Boatriders

The Juryman

Donald MacKenzie

An Orion book

Copyright © The Estate of Donald MacKenzie 1957

The right of Donald MacKenzie to be identified as the author of this
work has been asserted in accordance with the Copyright, Designs and
Patents Act 1988.

This edition published by
The Orion Publishing Group Ltd
Orion House
5 Upper St Martin's Lane
London WC2H 9EA

An Hachette UK company
A CIP catalogue record for this book is available from the British Library

ISBN 978 1 4719 0561 2

www.orionbooks.co.uk

For Ruth, with love

CHAPTER I

HE WOKE suddenly, stretching a hand to the bedlamp with a feeling of uneasiness. His watch, on the table beside him, showed a quarter to six. He lay, unmoving, establishing the familiar contours of the room. The closet where his clothes hung—the wash-basin—the French windows that led to the balcony.

The door to the sitting-room was ajar. He swung his feet to the floor and trod on shirt, underclothes, that were where he had stepped out of them, the night before. Sleepily kneading cropped black hair, he leaned against the wall at the door, listening. From behind him, rain pelted the long windows. Nothing else stirred. Irresolute and disturbed, he sniffed like a dog a couple of times then went back to the bed. Nerves, he thought, switching off the light. Since this case had started, he'd seen a cop in every doorway, a threat in every outstretched hand. He yawned once more, pulling the sheets about his ears.

He sat up quickly. This time, the rap of knuckles on his front door was unmistakable. Skin crawling, he waited. Again that insistent summons and the sound of movement from the landing outside. His pyjama coat was where he had thrown it during the night. He picked it up and hurried his arms into the sleeves. He called from the sitting-room door.

"Who is it?"

In the darkened room beyond, he waited for an answer.

"It's me, Mrs. Kolmer. It's a telegram, Mr. Steel."

"Christ!" he said with feeling. "Why can't they phone

it through? Banging on doors, this hour of the morning," he grumbled. His mouth sour for the housekeeper, he thumbed the catch on the door.

A square shoulder caught the hinged wood, throwing it open. There were three of them out there. Sombre faces under black Homburg hats and wearing the raincoats almost a uniform with the Metropolitan Police. Beyond them, old and hideous in the half-light, the housekeeper creased her face in a whine.

"I *never* had anything like this happen in the house before . . ."

All three men were strangers. One of them half-pushed, half-patted, the crone to the stairs. "Don't you worry about it, Miss. Go on back to bed." They waited. One to the left, one to the right and facing him, the shortest. Like a conjuror, the one facing Steel made an economical pass, flashing a warrant card in his hand.

"Police. Is your name Gerrard Steel?"

Steel hitched his drooping pyjamas with one hand, holding the open door with the other. He moved his head in acknowledgment.

"We'd like a word with you, Steel." The short man's chin was square—his face all bone with quick, dark eyes. "Do you mind if we come in?" Without waiting for an answer, all three pushed into the room. "Detective-Inspector Bates," the short man said formally. One of the others touched the light switch and shut the door.

Steel's mouth had dried as if touched with aloes. He pointed at his pyjamas. "Is it all right if I get my robe?" Illogically, he wanted his bare feet in something—as if the flesh feared trampling.

Bates moved a hand and one of the others went through to the bedroom. He came back and threw the blue robe from the door way. Steel caught it automatically and wrapped himself in its warmth. "What's all this about?"

2

he asked. Twenty times in the past, he remembered, he must have used the same cliché in similar circumstances. Both sides observed conventional dialogue as if in some traditional pageant.

The cop at the bedroom door had a mean face. He moved closer, tossing his mackintosh at a chair. His aggressiveness a foil for the inspector's calm, he snarled: "*You* know what it's about, all right." He flexed his shoulders, limbering his arms like a fighter. "Don't come that innocent stuff with us."

Bates shut him up. "Sit down, Steel," he invited. "We don't want any of that. We're going to take a look round— you won't mind, will you?"

Sit down. Stand up. They gave you orders in your own house, he thought savagely. Almost certainly, they'd have a search warrant. Or, if the visit had been dreamed up in a squad car, rolling the early hours of the morning, they would find thirty cops at the Yard with the seniority required to sign a warrant. *And* backtime it.

"Do I have any option?" he asked.

"Not much," Bates said. "But we like to keep things pleasant. Do you want to see the warrant?"

"No," Steel said. The sickness that worried his stomach was lack of food, he told himself.

Dark eyes never left Steel's face. "You're supposed to be a sensible man, Steel," Bates said reasonably. He pulled an envelope from his pocket. It contained a few press clippings, a typewritten sheet and a couple of photographs. Even across the room, Steel could recognize the pictures. That blank stare into the prison camera, the legend and number that were pinned to your chest. Bates slid spectacles to his nose, improbably benign. "Thirty-eight years of age," he read. "Born in Montreal, P.Q. Five years active service with the R.C.A.F. Honorable discharge with the rank of Squadron-Leader." He held one of the mug shots with regretful fingers. "Since then, five convictions," he intoned. He read from the typewritten sheet. "Theft, Montreal, P.Q. 1947. Six months imprisonment. House-breaking, London, 1948. Twelve months probation. Larceny and house-breaking, London, 1950. Two years imprisonment. Stealing by means of a trick, Paris, France, 1953. Six months, one hundred thousand francs fine and made subject to an expulsion order." He took off his spectacles, memorizing the last item. "House-breaking, London, 1954. Bound over to keep the peace for twelve months. That you, Steel?"

Steel nodded warily. "That's me. This is 1956. You guys choose what to keep in your records. What's the matter with the last three years—didn't they please you?"

The young one moved easily from the door. He took a fistful of Steel's robe and brought it up under the chin. "Let's try keeping a civil tongue in our heads," he growled.

"How long have you been living here, Steel?" Bates had a pipe that cut Steel's empty stomach. As if he knew it, the inspector rammed the burning tobacco into the bowl with calloused finger then sucked and blew till he was satisfied.

"Three years," Steel said, shaking his robe free. He looked up at the cop who stood over him. "Drop dead," he said.

Grinning, the man chopped with the side of his hand to Steel's face twice.

"All right, Bob," Bates said wearily. "Steel's going to behave himself, aren't you, Steel?" It was as if the pair of them were discussing a matter of joint but trivial interest. "Three years," he repeated from behind his pipe. "That's since you went to work for Sullivan?"

"Since I went to work for Sullivan," Steel answered.

"You're pretty good friends, aren't you, you and

4

Sullivan?" It was the third cop, speaking for the first time.

"He gave me a job and I worked for him. He gave me a job when nobody else would," Steel said. "In my book, a guy doesn't cease to be a friend every time the police try to pin some phoney rap on him."

The clock on the mantel whirred, striking the half-hour. The inspector checked the time with his watch. "Half-past six. The hours you people make us keep," he reproved. "Now you're a sensible chap, I'm sure. We know you bought a Luger pistol in France, four years ago. Sullivan used it to shoot Kosky." He stood up. "Would you like to tell us where it is?"

Steel started to rise but the second cop pushed him back in the chair. Steel's mouth went small, but he stayed silent.

"A pity," said Bates conversationally. "Still, a little more evidence and I'll have you with your friend in Brixton Prison. On a conspiracy charge. But if you like to help us . . ." He lifted the pipe as if it were a wand that might protect Steel from danger.

Steel fingered the weals on his face. "Sure," he said. "I know just what you'd do for me."

Bates moved to the mantel. Spectacles back on his nose, he poked into an empty vase with interest. "One of your friends—one of Sullivan's friends—gave us the tip." He lowered his head, black eyes showing over the spectacle frames. "Not that I think you'd be such a bloody fool as to have that pistol here, two months after we've pinched Sullivan. But it's worth a try," he finished easily. His voice hardened. "Sit where you are," he ordered.

Lights were thrown in the bedroom, bathroom, kitchen. Each junior detective took a room while Bates stayed with Steel. Sucking hard on his pipe, the inspector contented himself with lifting a cushion here, the top to the radio, peering on the ledge of the curtained window.

5

Through the open door, Steel watched a growing pile of shirts, underwear and suits as drawers and closets in the bedroom were emptied.

His gums smarted where the cop had struck him. Licking the insides of his lips, Steel watched the man with hate. The detective was in the kitchen. Whistling the same tune, tonelessly, he tipped out the contents of a dozen bags and jars. Salt, flour, sugar made a mound in the sink. Inspecting each empty container with mock-gravity, he let it fall to the floor. He went into the bathroom. There was a *clunk* as the man stood on the lavatory seat, prising the top of the cistern.

For an hour, they ripped sofa cushions, turned tables upside down, pulled back carpets, testing the floorboards. Finally, the three men were in the sitting-room. Bates moved serenely through the chaos, at work on his second pipe. His scalp showed white through thinning hair as he bent at the fireplace. He sounded the chimney with a broom-handle. Wood rapped brick with a sound that reverberated. An irate voice bellowed from the flat beneath.

The hardfaced cop held the suit that Steel had worn the day previously. Stitches ripped as he pulled pockets inside out by the linings. "We ought to get jobs as car dealers," he said to his companion. "Fifty-quid suits—plenty money and easy hours."

"You finished in there?" the inspector asked him. There was soot on Bates' face, on his coat. He used one one of Steel's handkerchiefs to brush it off.

The heavy clock sounded half-past seven with a wheeze. All three men were sweating. "Are we going to take him with us?" The younger man seemed to enjoy the prospect.

"You forgot to look somewhere." The sickness had gone, leaving a dull ache at the back of Steel's eyes. Unable to resist it, he made a suggestion brutally coarse.

"It's as likely a place to find a gun as in a telephone receiver," he pointed out. "What are you going to do now?" he asked. "*Find*," he spat the word—"a bunch of keys that fit a house somebody screwed last week?" For nearly two hours, he'd sat in that chair watching them methodically wreck the place. Now his eyes were red-lined and his back hurt from holding the same pose. Words had no value unless they insulted.

Bates' face flushed. He walked over to Steel. "There's nothing I'd like better than to put you away for a long time." He controlled his voice with difficulty. "I know your kind too well. You're more dangerous than the scum you work for. All education's done for you is to give you a sneer for anything that's normal." He dropped Steel's soiled handkerchief to its owner's lap. "Every cop's crooked—every time one of you's pinched, it's a frame-up. I've been twenty-five years at this game, Steel. And if I had to use your ideas to get a conviction, I'd sooner the streets were lousy with people *like* you."

In the sudden hush, the voice from the flat below bawled protest again. Offhandedly, the young cop lifted a chair in the air and let it fall. As if by signal, the three cops went through to the bedroom and stood by the French windows. Bates jerked the handle. Outside, rain bounced from the balcony and the two stone urns where sad plants drooped. The inspector pulled the doors shut and came back to Steel.

"Don't worry telling me what your lawyer's going to do to me," he said heavily. "I've been threatened with the entire Law List at one time or another." He clapped his hat on. "And I'm *still* on the Force." He opened the door to the landing and the other two followed him out.

Behind them, Steel rammed home the bolt and stood with his ear to the crack. When the street door slammed below, he ran to the French windows, switching off the

7

light as he went. He went out to the balcony, crouching in the rain behind the stone supports. He counted the three men into the glistening Squad car. After it moved off, he stayed on his heels, the rain a river behind his ears, his bare feet soiled with sooty grime. Carefully, he inspected each terracotta porchway on the other side of Draycott Place. They were empty. Letting himself down, belly-flat, he groped with one hand in the urn nearest him. At elbow-length, his fingers touched metal. Scattering soil, he pulled out the mud-covered Luger.

He shut the French windows behind him and sat, for a while, on the edge of the bed, shivering. The pistol had been there for two months. Each passing week made bigger the certainty no cop would bother him. Then, there had been nobody who knew where he lived. It had been crazy not to dump the weapon, the night Sullivan had returned it. Memories had stopped him. Guns that came into court via dredging hooks or turned in by small boys with big eyes. Rubbed free of fingerprints, the rifling destroyed by firing a shell of too large a calibre, the Luger had seemed safer under his control. Now he was no longer sure.

Keys, change and personal papers were on the bedside table. His wallet had been emptied and its contents stacked in a pile. Uppermost—as if placed there in contempt—was Galt's card.

FELIX GALT—SOLICITOR AND COMMISSIONER OF OATHS
235, Grosvenor Street, W.1.
Tel: MAY 0098.

There was a pencil scrawl in Steel's writing: "3.15 tomorrow." He touched the switch on the razor, buzzing the stubble from his face. In the mirror, the mark of the young cop's hand still showed on Steel's cheek.

8

For eight weeks, now—ever since Sullivan's arrest—there had been few moments that Steel might call his own. There were five used car lots that had to be visited, each with its own set of problems. And Warren Street, where the car dealers crowded the sidewalks, their stock-in-trade parked in front of them. For a hundred yards square, that was a nervous world. One in three car dealers had a memory of a prison number. It showed in the heads that huddled over tea in the corner cafés—the readiness to listen—the reluctance to discuss. Before his arrest, Sullivan's walk west from Warren Street Station had been heavy with the importance his reputation carried. Feared rather than liked, he had a smile for those in favour, a couple of quid ready for thieves in good standing but fallen on hard times. For Sullivan there were two worlds—one that belonged to "our own" and the other. In the six or seven years that the ex-thief had been legitimate, his sympathies never wavered. Warren Street was a place to buy used cars at a price, not a place to buy friends. Once Sullivan was behind the walls of Brixton Prison, the heads that Steel met on his visits to Warren Street were mostly averted. But every day, the walk had to be made in search of stock. Then Brixton with the mad scramble to get to the jail in time for visiting hours. Sheila Sullivan, still numbed with her husband's arrest, in the car beside Steel.

His face smooth, he cut the tiny motor and blew the loose hairs from the shaving head. He chose a blue suit from the pile on the floor and dressed mechanically. Fifty-quid suits, that cop had griped. Yet it was a matter of time, Steel argued, till the guy was patronizing the same tailors as the men he hunted. A matter of time till he traded his authority for a wad of notes, backhanded to him in some discreet rendezvous.

When he had knotted his tie, he took another look at

the littered floor. The maid was going to wonder but ah, well! For the first time in years, she'd have something to talk about other than her husband's asthma. He scribbled a note, pinning it to the table with three half-crowns. There were two extra chores to be done to-day. The Luger to get rid of and Sullivan's lawyer to see. That meant that Sheila would have to go to the jail herself, that afternoon.

He brewed coffee and ate cereal using the top of the refrigerator as his table. The Detective-Inspector's quiet malevolence was a memory that worried. They'd been three cops, he thought, with no more than a secondary interest in Sullivan's case, yet the hostility had been obvious. The hint of a tip-off was probably no more than cover-up for a sudden hunch on the part of somebody at the Yard. Tying Steel to the Luger was easier. He had been carrying the receipt for the gun when the French police had arrested him. Interpol could have passed the information to the Yard. Much worse than that was the fact that the police now knew where he lived.

Bored with the last few mouthfuls, he let cup and plate slide into the mess in the sink. Then he ran water, wondering what made a cop a cop. Chance had it that he had parked the Zephyr twenty yards further up Draycott Place. The car was safe enough. Like thirty others, it was registered in the name of Sullivan's company. Just the same, from now on, he'd have one eye on the driving mirror. He'd have no more police visits, he was sure of it. They would be waiting for him to make some false move. If he did—the chopping swing of the young cop's hand persisted in Steel's mind. That and the certainty that, on merit alone, Sullivan would be crucified in this case. From the Commissioner down, they were gunning for him.

It was light outside. He opened the long windows to

rain that blew in gusts. Clear on the wet wind came the
nine o'clock blasts from the factories across the river.
He wrapped the Luger in a sock and put it in the pocket
of his stormcoat. He took the stairs slowly, ready for the
ancient tragedy queen who was waiting for him at the
bottom. From her face, it was obvious that he had been
demoted from Mrs. Kolmer's list of desirable tenants.

"You'll have to leave after this, Mr. Steel," she bridled.
"It's no good. We never had anything like it before and
what the owners will say, I don't know."

Among other things, he noted sourly, her teeth clacked.
"Ah, my callers," he said. "But you let them in—I didn't
want to see them. 'A telegram, Mr. Steel'," he mimicked.
"I'm a little disappointed in you, Mrs. Kolmer," he
reproved.

She wavered a little under his mocking grin. "I had
to—policemen in the house at my time of life." Dislike
wrinkled her nose. "And Colonel Buckley complaining
of the noise over his head. The other tenants, too."

He let himself down on the bottom step, sitting facing
her. One by one, he checked three fingers. "I'd forgotten
the other tenants," he said. "Miss Armstrong, student of
drama. Wasting her moronic father's money and screwing
every guy hard up enough to fancy her, filthy ankles
included. Colonel Buckley—"he affected to consider—
"maybe the colonel's out of season—he's stewed to the
balls every night." He made his voice confidential,
leaning over at her. Like a fieldmouse fascinated by a
stoat, she veered towards him. "The legation secretary,"
he whispered. "But then I've seen him coming out of your
bedroom at two in the morning."

She clutched the housecoat to her throat. "Colonel
Buckley," she called faintly. "Police."

He put two fingers to his forehead and pushed by her
to the street door. The weight of the pistol in his pocket

made the twenty yards to the car uncomfortable. Though that one oversize shell had ruined the gun for ballistic purposes, mere possession was an offence that could put him inside for months. And if one thing he was certain, unless he stayed free, Sullivan was a gone goose.

He sat in the car for a while, considering where he might dump the pistol. Simplest of all would be a fast twenty miles out along the A.30. A hole somewhere in the beech woods, a splash in some farmer's pond and the thing was done. But there was no time. On an impulse he locked the car then sprinted thirty yards to the King's Road. Where he was going it might be difficult to park.

He boarded a 19 bus. At Knightsbridge, he pushed his way off and made for the park. The tall, narrow houses stood elbow to elbow, backing the carriage way. He walked past the barracks, squelching the wet underfoot. Thirty yards away was a building with construction workers sheltering from the rain. Behind a hoarding rose a forest of steel girders. On the left, a park of idle machinery, halted by the weather. Bulldozers, cement-mixers, tractors. A gate in the hoardings was guarded by a timekeeper's office, now empty.

Steel went through, picking his way in the churned clay. Most of the hands were busy drinking tea from cans, crouched round braziers in temporary shelters. He rounded the machinery park, passed stacked sacks of cement. Once, a couple of men on a crane looked at him curiously but he kept going as if he had the right. In the unfinished building, planks ran the length of the flooring. Some of the cement, still green, showed rings of moisture near the walls. The dank, lime smell curling his nose, he shuffled along the plank. At the far end, he rested on his heels, prodding the cement foundation. It was still soft. There was no one around. He pulled the Luger from the sock and pushed it into the cement. With

12

the end of a pencil, he forced the gun down through the yielding mass. Then spitting on the surface, he worked it with the length of the pencil. Nothing showed. He wiped his hands and made his way out of the building. As good there as the Bank of England.

It was after three when Steel drove up Grosvenor Street and parked on the north side, twenty yards west of Galt's office. The wind-driven rain blurred the back window. He lowered a side vent and peered past the cars in front. Then back, towards the lawyer's office. Apart from a doorman, disconsolate under cape and umbrella, the sidewalk was empty. Automatically, he checked the other side of the street. Few braved the damp misery of the October afternoon and none to disturb him.

Pulling the collar of the stormcoat to his throat, he ran, hatless for the steps of number two-three-five. The street door was open. From its angle, he took one last look at the traffic. Satisfied, he climbed the red carpeted staircase to the second floor. There were two doors leading to a suite of rooms. On the nearer, a bright brass plate.

FELIX GALT—SOLICITOR
RECEPTION

Steel ignored this door, shook the blue coat free of moisture and tapped on the further one. A voice inside called, he turned the handle. It was a quiet room with none of the cobweb trappings of a city solicitor's office. A deep carpet stretched to the Adams fireplace. High against the panelling, a gilt clock ticked unobtrusively. A few law books—a slim writing desk—were Galt's only concession to his profession. In the rooms beyond, the most modern technical devices were at the service of his clients. It was a combination of elegance and energy that contributed to his success.

The lawyer heaved himself up on short fat legs and crossed the room, bobbing like a cork at sea. "Nice to see you, Gerry. I'm due at Bow Street in a half-hour." He waved a hand. "But you're always punctual."

"Always," said Steel, draping the damp coat on the back of a chair. He crossed to the window and lit a cigarette.

"You are," agreed Galt. "You certainly are." Pressing a button, he spoke into the box on his desk. "Don't put any calls through, Miss Oliver—not till I say so." He settled back, rolling the dark lapels of his coat with his thumbs.

As if, Steel felt, Galt were conferring some inestimable privilege. He mistrusted criminal lawyers from experience. It meant nothing to him that Galt's record of improbable acquittals was of concern to both police and Law Society. Nothing that Galt had handled Sullivan's business affairs for five years. Lawyers, like women, should get as few facts as would satisfy them and be trusted with none. Steel watched the play of the red-fuzzed fingers. When he was ready, he spoke.

"I went up to the jail yesterday afternoon. Sullivan said I missed you by minutes. What did you want to see *me* about?"

The fine, carved arms on Galt's chair creaked as he settled his body comfortably. "Money, Gerry. Nothing else. You're—as it were—the paymaster now, aren't you?"

Like most things about this man, the false geniality bothered Steel. " 'Paymaster's' overdoing it. I use the company's money to pay bills whenever Sullivan tells me to." He blew smoke from the *Gauloise* and stubbed the butt. "But I don't have to agree with him."

Galt waved a conciliatory hand. His voice was almost apologetic. "I know exactly how you feel, Gerry. But then neither you nor Sullivan realizes the position we're

14

in. The *dangerous* position, Gerry." He smothered an after-lunch burp with mannered hand. "No. The pair of you are still thinking in terms of saving money and you can't do it, Gerry." He banged his desk top. "You're going to tell me you think Clarke's fee excessive," he accused.

Steel shrugged, running a hand through his black thatch. "Excessive isn't the word. It's a holdup. Up-to-date, this case has cost Sullivan twelve hundred quid. Before the first trial, you were all for Fox as a barrister. What a great pleader he was and the rest. I agree. At least he got a hung jury—why change him now?"

As if despairing of being able to explain, Galt wagged his large head. He threw a pink-taped brief across the desk. Pencilled on it was:

> Norman Clarke 1200 guineas plus two hundred guineas.

Galt worried his words as if faced with a recalcitrant witness. "That's the damage," he said. "And Clarke usually gets fifteen hundred without his junior's fee."

Steel tossed back the brief. "That tells me nothing except that Sullivan's got to find another fourteen hundred quid. For what?" he asked bitterly.

Galt scratched the back of his neck. "You're out of touch with the implications of this case. What do you think Sullivan will get if they find him guilty?" He leaned across the desk, waiting with interest for Steel's answer.

"Out of touch!" Steel's laugh was an unpleasant sound. "There's something you ought to know, Galt. I had a visit from the law this morning. A man called Bates from the Yard and a couple of others. Six o'clock this morning, with a search warrant."

"Looking for what?" Galt's voice was concerned.

"A gun," Steel answered.

15

Galt avoided looking at Steel. He toyed with the letter opener on his desk. "What did they find?" he asked.

Waiting till the other looked up, Steel gave him a cool stare. "What *could* they find? But they didn't leave any doubt about the implications of the case, as you call them. They told me precisely what they intended to do to Sullivan if they had the chance. Me, too."

The news silenced Galt. "You've nothing to worry about," he said at last. "There isn't a shred of evidence against you and they know it. Bluff!" he said largely.

Steel's head swung angrily. "Why don't you tell them that! There are plenty things I don't understand about this case, Galt. Either Sullivan's going to beat the charge or he isn't. For eight weeks you've been telling him—and his wife—that he was certain of an acquittal. Now it turns out he'll be certain if he can find another fourteen hundred pounds."

"There's no such thing as a certainty in a court of law," Galt answered. "I said he *should* be acquitted. If he isn't, he'll get ten years."

The voices of the clerks in the rooms outside were loud in the sudden silence. Steel looked beyond the wet windows at a sky that was grey and heavy. He lit another cigarette, giving himself time to think. Remembering that on a moor five hours to the west, four hundred men existed in captivity. Lived in a jail where the granite walls of the cell blocks dripped, dank in May. Dartmoor for a ten years lagging, he thought. With his record, Sullivan would be a marked man. Butt of countless petty tyrannies.

These past three years, Steel had been as close to Sullivan as anyone had ever been. From the age of ten, when he'd been sent to reform school, case histories, probation reports, the bored opinions of prison governors and chaplains, all had been building the picture of a Sullivan they recognized. "Psychopathic," "Ambiva-

16

lent," "This man expresses no regret for his anti-social behaviour." For years, they'd been telling Sullivan how hopeless he was, now there was tacit satisfaction when his conduct bore out their opinion. If they had ever recognized the man's fierce resentment of a world full of hate, they had sought to change the child rather than its world. The staunch, unswerving loyalty to those Sullivan had grown to think of as his own, went unnoticed.

Nights when they'd worked on the company figures, sunny mornings when even the weeds around the car lots made life easier, he and Sullivan had talked. The newfound respectability that had brought Sullivan comfort, a wife and a child, had given him a deep fear of losing them.

"I'd sooner take a rope, mate, than do any more time," Sullivan had said once. Steel had nodded. For him, there was no wife, no child to miss. Just the certainty that never again could he stand before a cell window and count the years to freedom.

Now, ironically enough, it was conceit instead of lust for possession that had landed Sullivan in this mess. But the end would be the same. A ten-year bit in Dartmoor would be Sullivan's death sentence. At the back of Steel's mind was the certainty that he alone could prevent it. If he could, he would.

"What sort of chance do you suppose that he's got with this new man?" he asked the lawyer.

The hand-made watch on Galt's wrist seemed to fascinate him. He played with the strap, considering. "Excellent," he said finally. "As a matter of fact, I lunched with Clarke to-day. While he hasn't studied the brief, he says that he's hopeful." The smile was large.

Hopeful! They patted your back, these lawyers, from the moment that you hired them till the jail gates shut behind you. And the bigger the fee, the better the production

they put on. "Sullivan's just another client to you, Galt,"
he said. "But he's a friend of mine. I want to know what
'excellent' means."

"A fifty-fifty chance." Galt poured reason into his
voice. "The Lord Chief Justice himself wouldn't go
further in a criminal case." He joined his short arms
behind his neck. Every gesture was made with plump
ease. "I know this is going to be his second trial, Gerry.
But it isn't completely in our favour that a jury didn't
reach a verdict at the first trial." He swivelled in the
chair, frowning. "We *always* knew the case for the prosecution. That first trial exposed our defence. There's
another thing. A jury's always swayed by the judge's
charge to them. This time, we're down for Court number
three." He shook his head. "That's Croxon. Croxon
trying a case with a weapon involved." He got to his
feet, and paced the width of the room, considering the
carpet. "*He* won't care whether the principals in this
case are both"—he found no better word—"undesirable.
I can hear him now. 'No one is beyond the protection of
the law.' If we go down, the sentence is going to be
exemplary."

Steel was a silhouette against the rain-splashed windows.
"You chose an odd time to spring all this on us. A couple
of days before the trial."

Galt stopped. He moved his shoulders briefly. "All this
newspaper publicity hasn't helped. Headlines talking of
gang vengeance and the like." He waved a hand with
derision. "We all know about the judge's admonition—
'You will pay no attention to anything you may have read
about his case.' And 'Consider this case solely upon the
evidence which you shall hear.' Balls! That's for earnest
young men in law school to believe. The complete
impartiality of the famed British justice! *We* know the
jury is going to be that more difficult to move in our

18

favour." He wrapped a heavy arm round Steel's shoulders, suddenly. "But if anyone can do it, Clarke can."

Steel lifted the arm and went to the desk. "You don't have to peddle your papers to me," he said with distaste. "Sullivan's already told me to give you a cheque."

As the other bent, writing, Galt touched the light button, making the room warm and friendly. "I'll get them to send your receipt. You know, you intrigue me, Gerry. There's no question about it—Sullivan couldn't have anyone better than you working for him outside. But you seem to refuse to accept the fact that I'm working for him too." He let his breath go, heavily.

"I'm paid for what I do, like you. But I try to earn my money." Steel grinned at the lawyer.

Galt took the cheque, professionally brisk. "That's it till Tuesday then. I'll meet you and Mrs. Sullivan in the main entrance hall at the Old Bailey. Ten-thirty. You know your way, of course."

Steel looked up sharply but Galt's eyes were innocent. Sure, he thought. He knew. And Sullivan's way, too. Handcuffed in a coach from Brixton Prison with no handles on the insides of the doors and an escort of six screws. "I know the way," he answered.

There remained something else that he had to ask. Something he had to be sure about, a possibility that had come with the shock of the early morning raid. "Suppose," he asked slowly, "the same thing happens at this second trial. Just one man on the jury who believes our story and eleven who don't. That's another hung jury?" Galt nodded. "Would they try Sullivan a third time?" Steel asked.

Galt was puffing into his topcoat. "As a matter of practice, no. The Crown will never offer further evidence where two separate juries have been unable to reach a verdict." Struck with the thought, he added, mock-piously: "Pray for just one rebel on the jury, Gerry. It'll be as good as an acquittal."

"If the new man does his job, we won't need prayers," Steel answered.

He went out to the stairs, the way he had come. It was dark in the streets and he watched the wet circles of light round the standards. The police were bound to know that he usually visited Sullivan in jail. After this morning, he could be sure that they would know all they wanted about the association. He buttoned his coat and went down the steps to the car. Now he knew what he must do, he could only hope that the police would let him alone. The best way, he and Sullivan would be walking the street in a few days time. The worst way, they'd both be giving their names in exchange for a number at Wandsworth Prison.

CHAPTER II

HE slammed the door of the car shut. He had to go out to Sheila's now. There could be no mention of what he hoped to do for Sullivan there. She respected the law and she feared it. That time they'd committed Sullivan for trial at the Magistrates Court, Steel had stood with her in the entrance to the West London Police Court. The two cops who were handling Sullivan's case had walked up. Big florid men with expensive clothes and a fondness for thieves' argot. The one called York had spoken.

"Hello, Sheila!" he said with the familiarity of the law for a defendant's woman. "How's Danny?"

20

Steel had watched as the blood left the girl's face. "Why not 'Mrs. Sullivan'?" he suggested. So there could be no mistake, he repeated. "To you, it *is* 'Mrs. Sullivan'." He nodded across at Galt who stood talking to counsel. "That's her lawyer over there. If there's anything you want to say, do it through him."

Sheila's nails dug hard in his arm and he felt her fright. "Please, Gerry," she said quietly. "You'll only make things worse."

York bulled his head into her face, grinning. "Don't worry, *Mrs.* Sullivan. He's not going to do anything foolish. We might send him back to Canada and he wouldn't like that. He's doing much better over here, handling Danny's money." She winced from the bad breath. "*And* his wife. Or did I say something wrong?" the cop asked.

It was nearly four by the clock on the dash as he filtered into the park and headed west for Chiswick. At Hammersmith, the rain had stopped, leaving the rows of cars at the Broadway traffic block glistening under the garish lighting. He bullied his way over to King's Street and made better time in the one-way traffic. It would be simpler if he reached the Sullivan home before Alan. Since Sullivan's arrest, Sheila's brother had been sleeping there. That fat lawyer had the nose of a vulture. Steel was sure that the last thing Galt expected was Sullivan's freedom. Even after the faint hope of the first trial, the West End was talking about Sullivan as one to be written off. A dead member. In ten years time, maybe, he would be welcomed with a big, big hand and a drink. Till then, the attitude was—ah well, that's the way the ball bounces!

He cut over at Chiswick Green, making for the quiet streets between there and the river. If this scheme ever climbed out of the dime novel class, he needed some sort of help. It didn't matter that a thief, strapped for a fiver, had always found Sullivan a soft touch. It wouldn't be among thieves that Steel would find help. None was to be trusted—not even with a package of contraband to be tossed over a wall.

Hating the need for help, as he resented all else that was criticism of self-sufficiency, he swung the wheel viciously. Piss-elegant houses for piss-elegant people, he mouthed, passing the tall, pretentious blocks of flats. In a section by the river, where small houses were surrounded with green and hedges, he turned into a dead-end. Tidal water slapped at the stone supports of the river embankment. There were lights in the house. He opened the garden gate and stood, listening. From inside, Sheila's voice sounded, calling her son.

He rang the doorbell, two long, two short. When you were news, the gentlemen of the press made no distinction between the home of a retired thief and that of a country vicar. This pre-arranged signal was the only one that Sheila answered.

Instinct told him that the quiet, country girl that Sullivan had married must know nothing of his plan. A woman's loyalty was always qualified by emotion. A man's was surer. For the help that he needed, Sheila's brother was a better proposition. It had been Sullivan's money that had given Alan the specialized training he needed, the kid's own brain that had made it worthwhile. Facts that Steel hoped neither forgot.

Somebody was fumbling at the lock on the other side of the door but no shadow showed against the ground glass panel. He flattened himself against the brickwork. Then, as a small coonskin-capped boy charged through the open door, Steel pounced.

He held the boy high in the air. "Boy, what a lousy hunter you'd make!" He swung the child to the ground.

"I'd have popped you a hundred times with my tomahawk."

He gave his coat to Sheila and, holding the boy by the scruff, followed her into the drawing-room. These past weeks, her shoulders seemed to sag—much of the steam had gone out of her, he thought. A coal and log fire threw warm patterns of light in the comfortable room. He flopped in a bright chintz chair. This was the kind of mess a convicted man left behind, he thought moodily. If he so far forget himself as to marry. Six days a week, Sheila carried food halfway across London. Then she talked to Sullivan for fifteen minutes through a grille and came back to this—without a single answer for a kid with a million questions.

His eyes followed Sullivan's child to the nursery door. No, he thought. Better the way *he* played it—a man was better off by himself If and when the law came, there were no tears—no hopeless lies. Just the hotel manager, worrying whether his bill would be paid.

He pushed his feet out to the fire. There was a sense of finality about being committed to Sullivan's aid. As long as it finished, Steel felt almost indifferent *how* it finished. He smiled welcome to Sheila as she pushed in the tea trolley. It was strange, the way people had these pre-conceived ideas about one another. If they sent Sullivan to jail, every evil-nosed old biddy in the country would be wagging her head over Sheila's picture. Maybe "gangster's moll" was too Broadway for England but it would be what they meant, all right. Yet to get her, Sullivan had had to promise much more than love, honour, obedience. He'd taken an oath never to break the law again. If Sullivan, riding the biggest coup of his career, had found it easy to swear, this was incidental. Till now, he had kept the promise.

Steel tweaked the girl's cheek as she gave him his tea

and was glad when she smiled back at him. For a while they sat there in silence, content with each other's comradeship. He watched the play of the firelight on the things that mattered to this grave, beautiful girl. The soft, silver teapot—the polished wood of the splay-footed table—the boy's picture. Through the open door, he heard the kid talking to Bella. He wondered vaguely how the maid had taken Sullivan's arrest. In all probability, secretly more outraged than a duchess. For the moment that you *felt* you had a position, you became anxious to maintain it.

"Gerry!" Sheila's voice startled him. Like an animal aware of danger yet uncertain of its source, he moved his head. "Gerry!" she reproved. "That's not like you— you've let your tea go cold."

He drank the brew without enthusiasm as she moved round the room, patting cushions, throwing wood on the fire. Maybe it was as well for her that she had a home to run—a kid to care for. At least, that way, she had less time to think. Unconsciously, he lifted his shoulders in incomprehension. If a man with a record *had* to marry, why in hell not pick one of his own kind! Especially Sullivan. Some hard chick with a memory of Pop in jail, a brother, or the man next door. *Somebody* who was—as they phrased it so delicately—"away".

"What time does Alan get in?" he asked suddenly. He kept his stare on the blazing pine. It was easier to lie with words than with eyes.

She held her hands to the flames, twisting the wedding ring. "Any minute, I suppose. Did you want to see him particularly?"

He recognized the curiosity in the soft country voice and told himself, careful! He lifted his feet casually, inspecting the mudflecked shoes. "No. It's just that the police are using pictures as evidence and I thought he might be able to give me the technical angles on it."

She went over to the nursery door and closed it. When she came back, she sat down facing him, her hands clasped. "I thought Danny looked better to-day—more relaxed. But he missed you, Gerry. He always misses you when you don't go up there." He made no answer. "Did you go to see Galt?" She was unable to suppress the anxiety in her voice.

He shifted his feet defensively, nodding. "I did. Look, Shee, I wish you'd stop worrying. You'll have us all climbing the wall. You're certainly making *me* nervous. All these meaning little phrases—I never saw anyone look so worried trying *not* to look worried. Galt's got a new barrister. A man called Clarke who's supposed to be one of the best Q.C.'s."

Her voice was both tired and abstracted—almost as if she had misheard everything he had said. "How long do you think they'll give him, Gerry—if they send him to prison?" Her fingers were still outstretched to the fire and they shook.

He threw both hands up, biting his words. "Christ knows why you can't spend your time more usefully than talking balls like that!! How many times do I need to tell you, Danny'll be back here next week. Sew buttons on his shirts! Darn his socks! How in hell should I know but stop crying on *my* shoulder!"

She blinked. "I know—I'm sorry, Gerry," she said submissively.

Oh great, he thought. Now the tears held bravely back. It was worse than if she'd howled in his face. "Sure," he said and touched her hand. "Sure. Just try and relax."

Footsteps sounded on the path outside and she said "Alan" and went to the street door.

Steel grabbed his coat and went after her. He called: "Hold it! Your lucky day," he greeted the man at the door. "You're having dinner with me."

The boy had his sister's grey eyes and serious mouth. Looking at him, Steel thought that Sullivan's money had been well spent. From the way the kid smiled to the way he wore his dark, well-cut suit, you couldn't fault him.

Taller than Steel, Alan bent his head to touch his sister's cheek. "Are you all right?" For ten years, each had had no more family than the other. Their closeness showed in the swift clutch of her hands at his shoulders, the smile he found for her. Alan gave Steel a hand. "Hello, Gerry!" Over his sister's head, he looked enquiry.

Sheila let him go and stood irresolute, as if warned by the same maternal instinct that both drew and repelled Steel. "Why can't I get you something to eat here? If you want to talk, I'll leave you alone in the drawing-room. You know I don't like being left."

"You won't *be* left," Steel said patiently. "You've got Bella, Tim and a telephone. And I'll have him back before nine." He shut the street door in her face.

The two men walked to the parked car without a word. Rain was falling again, clouding the lights on the towpath across the river. Inside the car, Steel turned on the heater, shivering.

"And how's the elegant world of fashion photography?" he asked. It irritated him, somehow, that Alan should be so untouched by his brother-in-law's arrest. He cupped his hand over a lighter flame.

The younger man threw his hat to the back seat. In the brief flare, he looked older than twenty-three. "I wonder you never grow tired of the sarcasm, Gerry. Haven't you *ever* been satisfied without cutting somebody to pieces with your tongue?"

Steel's headlights cut a shaft to the river. He let the motor idle. "Sure, I always forget your sensitivity. I want to talk about Danny." The darkness was cover for the

26

younger man's face. "It bores you, doesn't it?" It was impossible for Steel to resist the sneer. "You're starting to feel ashamed of your sister's husband. What's the matter, the models giving you a hard time about it?" The only answer was the drumming of Alan's fingers on the seat. Steel flicked ash, making the gesture an expression of contempt. "I can't remember any boredom on your part when Danny was paying your tuition fees, a couple of years back."

"Anything anyone has done for me, I've always repaid, Gerry." Alan was ignoring every challenge. "I'm not going to quarrel with you about that—or anything else. You know better than anyone else how I feel about Danny. But you don't consider the human element. You don't *want* to consider it—possibly you don't even recognize it."

"How many times have you been up to Brixton Prison?" Steel asked. Nobody knew, better than he, the uselessness of the accusation. The kid did a job of work, five days a week. Saturdays, there would have been a chance for him to go to the jail. It had been Sheila who stopped him.

"None," said Alan. "But if I thought it would do him any good, I'd be there every day. And you know it. Ever since we knew Danny, I looked on him as a sort of hero. It didn't matter to me *what* he'd been. If anything, it added to my hero-worship." He moved on the seat, coming over to Steel's side, touching his arm. "You know one of the first things I remember Danny saying to me— something that always stuck in my head? He said, 'Never mind about me, mate. It's your sister that counts in this family and don't you ever forget it! It's going to be rough on anybody who causes her unhappiness'." He took his hand from Steel's sleeve. "Do you know what's happening to my sister *now*? Don't *you* see what this is doing to her?"

It was strong, this impulse to tell the kid that he understood. The urge went back twenty years to a time when sudden warmnesses were not a sign of weakness. "That's what I wanted to talk to you about, Alan. Sheila, as much as anything. Christ, even I know that a man can't do what he wants to, always. Sometimes, he does as he must. And when that happens, a guy often needs help, not criticism. That's what's happened to Danny. What do you think Sheila will do if he gets ten years in Dartmoor?"

It was the space of a dozen doubts in Steel's mind before Alan answered, voice a little cracked with nervousness. "I don't think she'd want to go on living."

"Neither of them would," Steel said. Of Sullivan he was sure. Sheila?—women reacted dramatically, at times, to their husbands' imprisonment. There were the Splendid Little Women, resolved to make a tiny home for their men to come out to—to be waiting at the gate when the time came. The others whose grief, they thought, would send them head-first into a gas oven. Most times, life ground out the expedient solution. The Splendid Little Women made a tiny home—for somebody else. The gas oven brigade used it for cooking. No, Sheila may be hurt but it would be Sullivan who would surely die.

Steel reached to the dash and cut the headlights. They sat in the dark, the rain beating on the roof. "I'm going to give it to you straight, Alan," he said suddenly. "When I'm done, you can go back to Sheila. Danny's going to get ten years as surely as we sit here talking about it. That's unless somebody does something to help him. I'm not enough on my own, Alan. And apart from you, I don't know who to trust, to ask." He picked a shred of the strong tobacco from his lip, searching for a formula that would give the other the chance to back out without humiliation. There was none.

Alan moved restlessly, winding, re-winding the window. "I thought Galt . . ." he began. "Didn't that first trial

28

show that he may never get convicted at all?" he asked.
"I don't understand, Gerry," he said wearily. "It isn't
that I'm being difficult—ashamed of Danny. None of
those things. I just don't understand. I want to help him—
my sister—and lead an ordinary life. If I can't, I still
want to help them. You tell me how, Gerry."

"You better know it, Alan," Steel said soberly. "I'm
not going to wait for the police or some chicken-necked
judge to fix Danny." A barge horned, far-off, disquieting
him the way a plane did, leaving the tarmac. The sight
of a ship bound for some foreign port. He dragged deep
on his cigarette. "I'm going to take a crack at one of
the jury."

Alan's voice was still nervous but without drama.
"You mean bribe one?"

"Bribe. Bulldoze. Who knows," said Steel. "But
I know that among twelve people, *one* can be reached. If
things go sour, I'll finish up inside with Danny. If I swing
it, he'll go free. It's a chance I'm ready to take."

Alan was curious. "But how do you start on a thing
like that? I never heard of a juryman being fixed—not in
England, anyway."

It was stuffy in the car and Steel opened the side vent.
Beyond the dripping hedge, lights burned in the Sullivan
house. He shrugged. "I don't know. And in any case
I can't do it alone."

"You can count on me, Gerry," Alan said simply.

Now, for the first time Steel felt a little confidence.
He'd see that the kid came to no harm. But for one man,
alone, to start up an alley as dangerous as this was stupid.
Some help he had to have. There wasn't a man living who
couldn't be moved somehow. By fear, maybe. Cupidity—
compassion. But moved, if you went at it the right way.
Jurymen were still people.

He put an arm roughly round the other's body. "You

better get back to Sheila." Her name made him remember. "Alan—for Crissakes don't let her get the first idea of what we're up to. Neither of them must know, Danny still less. Tell her I wanted to see you about the pictures the cops have taken. Then I went on to a date I'd forgotten. Tell her anything." The next day was Saturday. "You don't work tomorrow, do you?" The younger man's "no" was almost inaudible. "Then meet me in the little bar of the Royal Court at twelve-thirty. I might know my arse from a hole in the ground by then."

He kept the car there till Alan's silhouette showed clear against the glass panel of the street door. Sheila's voice was sharp in surprise, then the door closed. He started the motor and drove without lights till he was well past the house. Homeward, there was the end of the day rush to contend with. Four million people, all in a crazy race to get home and start living. Or maybe stop living.

He took the Fulham Palace Road, then east for a mile to the grim, hopeless hotels along the Cromwell Road. At South Kensington, he bore left and parked in front of the tall, red brick house.

BELTON SERVICE SUITES

the lighted sign said. Home, he thought. All three rooms of it. With any luck, the maid would have cleaned around the place a little. Home. Time was when the word meant more, possibly. But it had gone—like the memory of the first frost in the maples, Santa Claus, the thrill of a pony race. You grew out of them.

He stood on the dark hall carpet, waiting for Mrs. Kolmer's door to open but this evening she disappointed him. He could be certain that she would ensure that dust was left in his rooms, his laundry forgotten and the 'phone messages garbled. The Old Bailey next week would decide whether he found another place to live or whether the Prison Commissioners did it for him.

He shut the door and stood for a while surveying the tidied room. Deep-seated habit made him inspect each familiar object, looking for a sign that might mean danger. Not necessarily from the cops. From anywhere. The world was a jungle. Yet for the past three years, he'd spent his time like most other people. Making his personal compromise with the business of getting through the next day.

That was something again—they were so goddam sure that you'd never change. Not only the professional Cassandras—the penologists and students of criminology but your grocer, the man who sold you a paper at the corner of the block. Any time a guy took a fall and landed in jail they said "They *never* learn, boy! They *never* learn!" And looked smug. The more bromidic came up with the dreary old crack "A leopard never changes its spots." If ever you'd been in jail and went back, they always knew it would happen. If you didn't, they said "Time will tell" and went back to rigging their accounts. They had it both ways.

He drew the curtains in front of the French windows and fixed himself a drink from the cupboard. Rye whisky and dry ginger. The fierce sweet taste was good in his mouth. Well, those bums were wrong—dead wrong. It was simple—all you had to do to make a thief honest was give him a reason. A reason that he understood. Sullivan, for instance. Sullivan would never steal another nickel. Since he had anything to lose, he'd been as keen as any *bon bourgeois* to keep it.

He skidded the chunk of ice round his glass, relaxed by the liquor. His own reason for keeping straight these past three years was even more basic. Nothing more or less than fear. He knew that the signs still showed. The chill

31

at the back of the neck when the doorbell rang, unexpectedly. The involuntary appreciation of a beautiful
ring on a woman's finger. The skeleton of the perfect
coup that glowed at the back of his mind. But society
wanted more from you than merely staying out of jail.
It wanted breast-beating. Snivelled aspirations to higher
things. The hell with it. Because he was afraid, he'd
worked hard, if for good money. What happened if some
judge blew both job and Sullivan to high hell was a
problem that must resolve itself.

He stirred himself to prepare a meal. He had no heart
for the gloomy caves along the King's Road where
decayed gentlewomen allowed one to buy coffee and tired
hamburgers at exorbitant prices. There was a slab of
steak in the refrigerator. He scored it with a razor blade
then kneaded pepper into the cuts. As he watched the
meat change colour under the grill, he remembered it
would be better than Sullivan had eaten that night. It
was almost eight o'clock. They'd have been in their cells
in Brixton since four o'clock. Now he could ask himself
why he would risk all that for Sullivan—for anyone. The
answer wasn't easy. Gratitude to a man who had helped
when no one else would? That, possibly, but that couldn't
be all. As basic was the certainty that he would help
Sullivan because he must.

It was nine when he put out the lights and sat at the
open windows. The rain had settled to a fine drift that
clouded the street lamps on the other side of the street.
The smell of Miss Armstrong's supper came from upstairs,
creasing his lip and nostrils. He'd had some. Spaghetti,
cheap red wine and Miss Armstrong's account of her
tragic life, all twenty years of it.

A cop in a cape passed by, below, scanning the parked
cars. Pretty soon now, Steel remembered, he'd be back
in that half-forgotten world. Squad cars, immobile on

some quiet street, black glass in the rear windows and behind it the cops. It didn't matter whether you were clean or not—innocent of purpose or caught with a pocketful of hot jewellery. A thief had to seem more innocent than a minister of the gospel. From somewhere, you had to find the right combination of walk and expression—and the nerve to carry it past the parked car. He was committed to a world of tapped shoulders, furtive mouths, wary eyes. And he was afraid.

Sullivan came into the picture, three years before, a couple of weeks after Steel had stood, that last time, for sentence. Up and over his right shoulder, the peaked faces of the sensation-mongers leaned from the public gallery of the Central Criminal Court. Each side of him, the two jailers were fatuous in their attempts at the right appearance of zeal. Down below, his lawyer doodled on a pad.

The scene was set and the audience ready. All through the trial, Steel had used a bald-headed man on the jury as a sort of barometer. He'd tried to gauge the man's reactions as the prosecuting attorney made his points. Once, it had seemed, the man looked at Steel with a smile, as if half in sympathy. When the jury came back with a verdict of guilty, the guy avoided his eye till the foreman spoke. Then he glared at Steel with open disapproval.

That dock with its glass surround had been a lonely place. He waited for the sentence to be given so that he could return to the steel and tile box below. With conscious bravado, he pulled his shoulders back and concentrated on the emblazoned coat-of-arms that hung over the judge's head. This horsefaced old man was almost certainly going to hand out the years spliced with sniffling platitudes. All judges loved it. All of them had to smother their secret doubt, justify their own savagery.

Steel had looked up at the old man who, hunched on

the bench, wrote in painstaking longhand. When the judge was done, he passed the form down to the Clerk of the Court and leaned on both elbows. He emphasized his words with a spectacle case. It was a thin, cultured voice, hollow in the microphone and completely dispassionate.

"You've had a long trial, Steel, and have been found guilty. Very rightly so, too, I should add. Both from your general attitude and your demeanour in the witness box, I gather the impression that you are completely indifferent. Not only to the judgment of this court but to that of your fellow men."

The judge waited for a redfaced cop to retrieve a bunch of keys that had clattered to the floor from the exhibit table.

"You've shown yourself to be a skilful, determined thief since you arrived in this country from Canada. Pure luck and the good work of the police officers prevented you from getting away with it this time. Quite properly, your counsel—to whom you owe a debt of very real gratitude has put before me certain matters in his plea in mitigation." The judge took his spectacles from his case and considered the papers in front of him. He went on. "He says that you have never had a chance." The intimacy of his tone was salt in a gash to Steel. If only the old bastard would get it over! "But a chance is exactly what you *have* had," the judge said mildly. "Almost too many, one might suspect. From the moment you were born." His voice was suddenly clear. "You're a fool, Steel. In spite of the psychologist's report, I say you're a fool. I'm in some doubt whether the action I propose taking in this case is the right one. You will be bound over in the sum of twenty pounds to be of good behaviour for two years." He paused. "But I want you to be very certain of one thing, Steel. If ever you have occasion to appear before a

34

court again, convicted of *any* crime, you will have an extremely unpleasant shock. I am marking your papers appropriately. Do you understand?"

The jailer's hand nudged Steel's elbow and he tried to say something. But nothing came till a croak, unnaturally loud. "Yes, m'lord. I understand."

He retrieved his belongings in the labyrinth below the dock. "Sign 'ere," said the bald-headed jailer who had been the quipster all the way from Brixton Prison. "That's the quickest five years *you'll* ever do, chum."

Steel took what money there was, his watch and ring, a few letters that his lawyer had written to him. He scrawled a receipt. "Save the humour for them," he said with dislike, jerking his head at the rows of occupied cells. "Maybe they'll appreciate it." Savouring the moment, he lit a cigarette, deliberately. "Now how do I get out?"

The jailer drew down the corners of his mouth, cocking his head at his partner. "Always in a 'urry, aren't they, Jim. You'll be back, chum, you'll be back."

"Sure," said Steel. "To keep bums like you in a job. What would you do otherwise—open cab doors?" He went up the stairway to the dock then down to the well of the court. This was the pedantry of the legal mind, he thought. If they set you free, it had to be through the dock that you'd stood in.

Then you were outside the Old Bailey. Suddenly a whole way of living apart from the men you'd left in the cells inside. All these people passing had long since compounded with society's rules. It was an odd feeling. Twenty minutes ago, found guilty and prepared for a sentence—free, now, to do what you wanted. That old man in a wig had showed mercy. Steel didn't know why— resented, in a way, the tacit obligation under which it placed him. Resented the itching uncertainty that, possibly, the Square Johns were right—the clerks, the bum at the corner with a tray of balloons—even the tall-helmeted City cops at the court entrance.

He walked round the corner and waited for a bus that would take him back to his hotel. If they *were* right, now was the time to find out. It was too easy, waking in a whitewashed cell, to fool yourself with resolutions what you'd do when the great day came. Too easy to spend years in jail planning a return to society that was based on the world standing still, applauding.

He had seventeen pounds. The hotel manager returned his few good suits in exchange for most of it. Two weeks, it took, for Steel to understand that an ex-Squadron Leader with a couple of medals and five convictions for theft was expendable. For a dozen days, he was first in at the Public Library, scanning the Help Wanted advertisements in the morning papers. As many as he could, he tried. There were regrets, curiosity, embryo sermons that he'd cut short but no job. Had he been the sort of ex-convict employers reognized, it might have been different. As it was, people shied from a problem they did not acknowledge.

It was a fine afternoon in a bar off Baker Street and Steel had been down to the last couple of quid. The whisky blurred all thought of where the next money might come from. Then Sullivan walked in.

A few years before, they had done a sentence together. Since then, Steel had never seen the man whose share in the unsolved Braden Bullion Robbery had produced thirty thousand pounds for him and a mint-condition resolution that crime was for suckers.

"All right, mate?" Sullivan's easy recognition was that of the successful thief for the unsuccessful one.

Any other time, personal conceit would have forced a nod from Steel as easy as the other's offhand production of another drink. This was different. Sullivan's conversion to respectability was a matter of irritation to the still-smarting cops, of resentful jealousy to the thieves he had worked with. It pleased nobody but Sullivan and the newspaper men who made as much of it as they could without pinning a libel suit on themselves.

"It couldn't be worse, Sullivan," Steel said. He cleared his head with an effort, pushing away the drink Sullivan had bought him.

"Get the winter over, mate, and it'll be easier," said Sullivan. "With the dark nights. You're too good a screwsman to go hungry." Without making a show of it, he reached a hand to his wallet and started pulling out money.

The dark nights, thought Steel. The swift silent entry into a flat—the smooth feel of jewellery in your hand that you'd watched for weeks on the fingers or neck of some unsuspecting woman. It could be like that for two hundred dark nights till some incalculable factor appeared. The unnoticed face at a window, the call to the Yard, the corners and doorways that spewed cops as you made your way out of the burgled flat. And when that happened, that old judge had told you, there would be an unpleasant shock. In that bar and at that instant, he knew that he could never serve another sentence in jail.

"I want a job, Sullivan. If you'll give me one, you won't be sorry." He moved away from the inevitable drunk being everybody's friend and stood next to Sullivan. "This is on the level," he insisted. "I need a job."

"Why me?" The mere beginning of a grin showed on Sullivan's face.

Because he needed them, Steel's wits were sharp. Sullivan's readiness to help was genuine enough—but much of the time his need was as big as the people he helped. Sullivan needed substantiation of his own image—

the picture of himself that he lived with.

Steel was able to give it to him, truthfully. "Because there's nobody else who'll give me one," he said. Desperation gave him the words. His arrest, the trial at the Old Bailey, the search for a job. He made the account bald, without drama, the way that he sensed the other might have told it. "I can't do any more time, Sullivan." With the compulsion that jerks that last nickel from a thief's pocket, he called for another drink for Sullivan.

"Be lucky!" Sullivan finished his beer and leaned on the bar, massaging his temples. The gesture was theatrical but Steel took heart. "What I *need*, mate," said Sullivan, his eyes on the glass in front of him, "is someone who wants to keep out of the nick. And means it. And someone who can rabbit—not just one of them false-pretence talkers from the clubs round Chelsea. They're not worth a shit, the lot. But you've got a bit of class." He looked up at Steel, suddenly, his eyes hard. "I never heard nothing against you, mate." He put out a hand. "Neither of us is too 'ealthy with the law. And this is a dead straight business I've got. I want it to stay like that. Understand?"

Steel took the firm fingers. "You won't regret it."

For three years, it had been like that till a few weeks ago. Each had honoured the other's interests. Because he must, Steel would continue.

He went back into the bathroom and washed. Better hitting the sack at nine than sitting there in the dark. Knocking yourself out with the thought that in helping Sullivan, you jeopardized everything you'd gained these past years. If he wanted, the city outside held no excitement that he couldn't explore. And here he was, getting ready to thumb a nose at the man who had given him a break that was even more important than the one Sullivan had provided. The memory of that thin, old voice at the Old Bailey persisted into his sleep.

He pulled the covers round his neck. You couldn't be loyal to opposites, not at the same time, you couldn't. Even if it were desirable. Honesty—justice. Twenty-four hours a day, they bawled these moral principles from press, parliament and pulpit. But what they really meant was expediency.

He slept as he always did, ready to wake to a world that was worse than it had been the night before.

CHAPTER III

HE was up, bathed and dressed and on the street before the house stirred the next morning. He had hot black tea and limp toast in a café filled with caped guardees from the barracks opposite. From nine till twelve, he sat a hard chair in the Reference Room of the Chelsea Public Library. Across the broad reading table, a Nigerian in a striped cotton robe recited civil law to himself. Pimpled students from the Polytechnic next door agonized over chemical formulas. Occasionally, an old wretch in for shelter ruined the silence with an involuntary belch.

Steel had a dozen books at his side, from *Whitaker's Almanack* to the *Juryman's Handbook*. The careful notes he had made were reduced to a few lines that he committed to memory, throwing the slips of paper into the trash basket. Outside, a pale clear sun shone. He walked the length of the King's Road, obliged to shove through the knots of sloppy shoppers clogging the sidewalks. In the tiny bar at the top of the stairs at the hotel, Alan was waiting at a table. The other two tables were empty.

Steel took a chair and regarded Alan without too much

enthusiasm. There had been a noticeable shake as the younger man's fingers had come outstretched across the table. Nor did Steel miss Alan's nervous stare at the swinging door to the street. He ordered, making small talk till the drinks came. Alan would settle down, he hoped. It was the essential difference between the amateur and the professional, both cold-bloodedly contemplating crime. Both might be scared but only the amateur would show it.

With the first drink of the day, Steel's shoulders were big and his mind a bright light in a dark room. He kept the tone of his voice deliberately casual. "What'd Sheila have to say?"

"Nothing. Just 'Oh! you're back early!' That's all."

Through the curtained glass in the restaurant, a few couples were making an early lunch. The bar was deserted and the barman bored. Steel pitched his voice so that it travelled no further than it need. "Short of getting at the summons sent out by the Under-sheriffs, there's no hope of telling who'll be called for jury service at any time. Let alone for any particular case. As far as I can see, the whole thing's a lottery. If I'm interpreting what I've read correctly, you can live a lifetime in London and never get called. Then again, maybe a summons'll hit you the moment your name shows on a voter's list."

Alan was listening with his head down, making small circles with the bottom of his glass. At Steel's insistence, he looked up. "So I've got to start looking right there in open court." Alan still looked blank. And even to his own ears, Steel's scheme sounded no more than a thin bleat of hope. Somehow, certainty had to be injected into this kid. Steel rapped for two more drinks. "It'll be done, Alan," he said. "That's for sure. We've got to work fast and use our heads. One thing—I never want you near the court building, do you understand?"

40

The creases between Alan's eyes smoothed and he grinned weakly. "Whatever you say, Gerry." His relief was pathetic.

Steel followed it up. "You're just the boy in this deal—don't forget it. Fetch and carry, that's your job. From start to finish, there's no earthly reason why you should see a single cop." He felt his ascendancy and leaned across the table. "Keep your evenings free, that's all. Every single evening, whether I want you or not." He winked. "They'll wait."

"What about Sheila—she'll ask questions?" Alan was dubious again.

Suddenly impatient, Steel said: "What do you want—a liar's manual. Your sister isn't any different to any other woman, Alan. She'll believe what she wants to believe, given the chance. *You* work it out. Just be ready when I phone."

Alan drained his glass. "All right." He hesitated. "I thought of going up to Brixton this afternoon, with Sheila."

Steel shrugged, threw coins on the table and got to his feet. "If you do, for God's sake keep off the subject of how long Danny will get. And tell him that I'll be in court on Tuesday morning. Just that."

They went out separately. The smell of food in the hotel had put back appetite into Steel. He went back to Draycott Place and fixed a meal. For two days now, since he'd taken his decision, he was happier alone. It was the recurrence of a rhythm of behaviour grown unfamiliar through disuse. The uneasiness in the daylight street—the straining for sounds at night. He was beginning to remember the involuntary feeling of surrender that went with the commission of every crime. A black echoing tunnel that you travelled with growing doubt.

That afternoon he went over to South London and

bought crêpe-soled shoes, strip celluloid, hacksaw blades, files and a tiny vice. In a back street Battersea locksmith's, a man with a cap and broken teeth sold him a dozen key blanks with scepticism.

" 'ere y'are, guv. Find what you want 'ere, you will."

Steel left the store, resisting the urge to turn and face the stare that bored his back.

Back in Draycott Place, he worked slowly, the small vice fastened to the kitchen table. Cutting and filing the blanks to basic raised or dropped patterns. It was after midnight when he finished. Cramped fingers and skinned knuckles betrayed the lack of practice. He'd cut three keys—the rest he'd do before Tuesday.

Now he oiled the three pieces of metal and wrapped them in a wad of cotton. It would be a crude kit, even when he finished, but with the 'loid, he'd have an even chance of an entry. From the time the jury was sworn, he had to be able to go where he wanted, without benefit of permission.

Sunday was hideous with church bells, morning and night. Most of the day, he stayed in bed with the radio on at volume. Mrs. Kolmer's door rappings he ignored. After dark, he walked in the new crêpe-soled shoes, secure in their silent tread. The length of Sloane Avenue, past the cluster of hospitals to the back reaches of unfashionable Chelsea. Twelve strangers he kept remembering, and he had to choose the right one. A man who wouldn't yell "Cop" as soon as he was tackled—a man with more heart or need than social conscience.

At Stamford Bridge and the Dog Track, he turned back. Half-a-mile north, the bars of a dozen pubs would be stiff with professional thieves and their wives. Sunday night when their women sipped Guinness socially and appraised the finery of the others. The boys talked it up at the bar over large scotches. There were few of them who hadn't

been befriended in some way by Sullivan in the past.
A tenner, maybe, towards the cost of defence or a few
quid in the man's hand at the jail gate. If you blew up
that picture to include Belgravia inns and Hoxton barrel
houses, the pattern held good. Yet now, there wasn't one
who'd give Sullivan the time of the day. Theirs was a
world where you were remembered just as long as you
breathed. And for them, a man in jail stopped breathing.

He cut down Sidney Street, past the back of Saint
Luke's churchyard, ready for bed.

Monday morning, there were chores to be done—
too many for the hours to register. He set about them with
the fatalism of a man who surrenders to his bail. At his
bank, he took fifty pounds in cash and transferred the
balance to a deposit account. He left a formal notation
at Canada House that he might be away for a while.
There was no need for any explanation elsewhere. If he
dropped out of sight, there'd be four or five women who'd
ring his number a couple of times. Then a pencil would
go through his name in the little book. He thought of packing most of his clothes in cases then remembered the love
of a cop to peek. There'd be ripped mattress covers, up-
heaved carpets, broken furniture, if he were
arrested. Ah well, Mrs. Kolmer would have fun
again.

He rang Galt and Sheila, confirming the meeting time
for the next morning. Later that night, he drank two
bottles of champagne in a Soho cellar. At one o'clock he
detached himself from the inevitable vicar's daughter,
trapped by one foolish fancy, and took a cab back to his
rooms.

Awake at seven, he made his breakfast without haste.
Many of his actions were seeming instinctive. The choice
of the dark grey suit, conventional both for appearance in
court and burglary. The flat package he made of the

43

twelve finished keys and celluloid strip and tucked into a hip pocket.

As he went out, Mrs. Kolmer was waiting. Old, cob-webbed eyes and brilliant false teeth. Lifting her shoulders, she drew breath. "I have instructions to receive no further rent from you, Mr. Steel. Your tenacy is termin-ated as from the end of this week."

"*Tenancy*," he corrected. He pushed by, taking the letters from the hall chest. There was none for him. "That's great," he went on. "You can find somebody else to haunt."

She backed to her door, holding the dingy housecoat high at her neck. "You *ruffian*!" she said. "I heard—he'll get it—that friend of yours! Crooks, the lot of you!" She slammed the door.

He pictured her on the other side, heart hammering and one ear at the wood.

The easy way to the Old Bailey was south to the river and along the embankment. In the city, he went north. Parking wasn't simple, he realized. As usual, the police had cluttered the space in front of the court building. There was a bomb-site beyond, with ample room, but he wanted to leave the car where he could move out in a hurry. Another thing, he wanted to be able to watch the exits—all save two were on the front of the building. These were of no interest to him. Already a queue was forming at one—the Public Gallery. The other was a facility exit for judges and counsel.

It was just after ten-fifteen. He drove across the main thoroughfare and rounded Smithfield Market. The circuit took ten minutes. By the time he reached the lavatories in front of the Old Bailey, a police car was pulling out. Steel rammed the Zephyr into the vacant slot.

For a while, he sat there, eyeing the people who

climbed the main steps. They were readily identifiable. Barristers, black-hatted and showing white wing collars and white bands under their coats. Hard-eyed cops, carrying bundles of exhibits and bulging document cases. The friends of the prisoners, embarrassed and apprehensive, ducking up the steps with their heads down.

By now, Sullivan would be deep in the bowels of the building, in a cell twice the size of a phone booth. He'd stay there till the case was called. Steel found no rancour in the thought. For years now, he'd observed the business of crime and punishment with some objectivity. Only the word "justice" he refused to accept. This goddam abstract idea that was draped over all law enforcement activities, ennobling their own crimes. Had they for "justice" used "expediency" . . . he shrugged.

He rid himself of the package of keys and strip, hiding it under the floor carpet. Then he locked the car and followed the crowd to the top step of the steep stairs. Double glass doors insulated the marbled hallway from the raw day. Ahead, a broad stairway forked left and right to the second storey and the Court entrances. This lobby, with its busts, spotless floors and attendants, bug-eyed with vicarious importance, was like that of a continental opera house. Four notice boards held printed sheets with the cast of the day's performances.

The roles of court attendants, guardians of the exits, keepers of order within the court precincts, were played by the City of London Police. Technically, every prisoner in the building was in the charge of the prison governors, and prison warders locked and unlocked in the cells below, stood in the dock as escort.

Aware that one of the helmetless cops was watching, Steel bent at the board.

COURT 3

CROXON, J.

R. *v.* Hanningan, R.   (For sentence)
R. *v.* Lowrey, J.   (For sentence)
R. *v.* Dunn, L.   (For sentence)
R. *v.* Sullivan, D.

The cop was young and still civil. "Are you looking for something in particular, sir?"

"I just saw it—" Steel answered. "Court 3."

"That's upstairs and on your left. Very interesting, it could be. It's that attempt murder case. Man called Sullivan. I expect you've read about it." He was a simple fellow and the thought showed plainly in his face. "Are you a friend?"

"That's right. I'm a friend of Mr. Galt, a solicitor in the case." There was no reason for the cop to know him and still less reason to volunteer information. Already, the thought of that old man upstairs made his stomach rumble. He'd be sitting there like a waxwork—listening without moving—pale, washed eyes that you'd swear could see no further than the committal papers in front of him.

The cop nodded. "You'd better tell the officer on the door that you're a friend of the solicitor. Otherwise he'll send you round to the Public Gallery. That's full, a case like this."

Doubtless it was. There'd be the usual bunch of bums in for the warmth, the professional court visitors—for the most part thin-lipped and old, enjoying the substituted sense of power. Then the Elders of the underworld; so called. Agog at the prospect of two prominent rascals— one active, one retired—appearing in court as prosecutor and defendant. It was a tit-bit for such of the boys as might summon the nerve to sneak into the Public Gallery. Visiting courts, like visiting prisons, was usually an item on a thief's "DON'T" list. Together with being seen with a man unpopular with the police, or being the last to talk to a guy before his arrest. All weakened the sense of security that a thief had to have, no less than anyone else.

The second floor was a replica of the first. Metal busts of bygone judges, noble precepts cut into friezes and an incongruous pair of telephone booths. Polished wood benches, back to back, ran the length of the hall. Here the crowd was divided into constrained groups— factions, almost—like the adherents of York and Lancaster in a village pageant. On one side, the prosecutors, Crown witnesses, solicitors. On the other, defence witnesses and prisoners' friends. The last showing markedly more hostility in their attitude. Here and there, a cop crossed the floor, unconvincingly neutral, to whisper in someone's ear.

Galt was standing with Sheila at the far end. Past them, counsel, already gowned, were grabbing a final cigarette before going into court. Sheila wore black with no jewellery except her wedding ring. Her fine-boned face was still pale, her eyes uncertain, but she managed a smile as she saw Steel.

The fat lawyer, dapper in dark blue suit and polka-dotted bow-tie, was jovial. "Dead on time, as usual," he greeted. "Well done." He moved his fingers discreetly, wiggling them close to his stomach. "Over there," he whispered. "That's Clarke." With no sense of the outrage he committed, he added: "The other one's Trelawney. He's prosecuting."

The urbane legal etiquette angered Steel. Two men playing Dear Old Pals when in a while they'd be arguing for a man's liberty. In court there'd be the vehement objection, the mannered sarcasms, but out here they were a couple of actors discussing their lines.

"I see them," Steel said shortly. "What time's it on?"

With some annoyance, Galt shrugged. "I was just

telling Mrs. Sullivan. Not before the afternoon, I'm afraid. There are three up for sentence—that will take the best part of an hour. Then Clarke has a motion to make before the jury is empanelled. And that will take time—choosing the jury, I mean." He picked at his red eyebrows. "I'll make sure," he said. He bounced over to the two barristers, like a fat puppy approaching a pair of elderly greyhounds.

Steel walked Sheila to the great windows. "How is he?" She was uncertain. "All right, I think. I saw him yesterday afternoon."

"Was there any message?"

She shook her head. "Nothing. I told him you'd be here to-day."

Away on the far side of the hall, Steel could see York and the other detective in the case. Past them, Kosky—still wearing a bandage though it was eight weeks since Sullivan's shot had nicked his hairline—the two cab-drivers who were giving evidence for the Crown, the other witnesses. Their own witnesses were grouped round Galt's managing clerk, listening with interest.

Holding Sheila's arm firmly, he propelled her up the hall. "You're going to have four or five days of this, Sheila. It won't be any shorter than the last trial was. You've got to relax and remember it's going to be all right." The banality of his words was plain, yet he could think of no others. As Galt tipped back, Sheila took a breath. "I'll be no trouble," she said quietly.

Galt threw both his hands out. "There it is. You can both go for a walk. Take her for lunch—a drink. It'll do her good," he told Steel. "We're not on till five minutes to two. The judge is recessing early, immediately after the jury is empanelled. They'll start the case this afternoon."

"I'll hang around," Steel answered. He couldn't leave! When those names were called, addresses given, he had

to be there. "That's all right with you, isn't it, Sheila?"
Neither did he want to sit next to her in court. It would be
too easy for her to see what he was doing with pencil and
and paper and wonder why.

"Of course." She was indifferent. "I'll find something
to do. I'll be back at five to two," she told the
lawyer.

Neither man spoke till they had watched her through
the crowd. Steel nodded at Clarke. "Is he still confident?"
he asked. The better the man was, the easier his own task.

Galt put his hand reassuringly on Steel's arm, his voice
velvet. "*Hopeful*," he said. "He'll be doing his best and
that's good enough for most." He went down the stairway
to the street.

Now that the doors to the courts were open, the crowd
thinned. Steel started for Court 3. It shouldn't be difficult
to find a seat near the jurybox yet out of sight of the
judge. All the witnesses in Sullivan's case had gone and
the business before that court was merely formal.

Suddenly an arm was pushed in front of him. He
looked up to see York. The detective's partner stood
slightly to one side so that between them, they were the
head of an arrow, blocking his passage. He moved to walk
round them.

York was breathing heavily, his face red and puffed
like that of an angry rooster. "Wait a minute. Police
officers. What's your name?"

Steel's surprise showed in a nervous swagger. "My
name? Steel. Yours is York. We've been introduced,
remember?"

If he looked for response, there was none. Without
taking his eyes from Steel, York spoke to his partner.
"What do you think, Jack?"

Like a farmer at a cattle fair, the man inspected Steel,
from the long narrow head to the black, wing-tip shoes,

"I think you've got the right one, Fred," he answered slowly.

Usually, police humour was about as subtle as a pair of brass knuckles. Maybe this was a sample. Both cops stared at him, deadpan.

"Don't you think you ought to cut this out!" he started hotly. He could feel the pumping surge of blood that accompanied fear. There was a menace that he recognized but was unable to identify. "I've got no time to waste." Again, he moved to go round the pair.

"You don't want a scene here, do you? Stay where you are." York meant what he said.

Steel stood still. The manoeuvre bore the earmarks of an arrest but he didn't know for what offence. There was that self-conscious purposeful look on York's face. Next would come the stylized language that pompously followed a pinch. "I am a police officer and am putting you under arrest."

He tried to stifle his apprehension. "You'd better tell me what all this is about—am I pinched or what?"

York made a heavy attempt at feigning amazement. "Not yet, chum, but you do answer the description of a man who jumped his bail, three months ago. Man called Grey. Your description to a T. That accent of yours is probably faked," he said.

It still made no sense. He tried to keep both temper and fear under control. "I wasn't on any bail and you know my name as well as I know yours. Something else, you know I haven't been pinched for three years."

There was a black broken tooth in York's upper jaw that showed when he grinned. A patch of dried blood on his adam's-apple bobbled as he spoke. "We can do something about that," he said jocularly. "I'm going to take you down to Hammersmith Police Station. You're not arrested, just detained." Taken with his own humour,

50

he clowned for his partner. "We're sorry to trouble you, but we've a job to do, sir.

Now he caught on. It wasn't an original manoeuvre, this one of York's, but a favoured gambit whenever a cop wanted to throw a scare into a man with a record, grown uppity or rich. A cop was within his rights in taking a guy to the station, detaining him on some pretext, then turning him loose after hours spent with the man stumbling for answers to questions he didn't understand. Chances were that this pair couldn't afford the time to make even a fast round-trip to Hammersmith Police Station. They had to be in court in the afternoon. But the possibility was still there. If ever they did pull him in and then turned him loose, they would be able to justify themselves. He was a man with a police record and they'd make their version of the affair convincing. They knew it—he knew it. And this was no time to put a cops' bluff to the test.

There was another gambit, equally simple, by which you avoided the inconvenience. "How much?" he asked.

York explored his nose. "If we had a tenner apiece, I think we'd be able to bet it on your name being Steel. Not this bloke who's jumped his bail. I think that's a fair bet, isn't it, Jack?"

"Very fair," agreed the other cop.

They moved further up the hall and into the privacy of the phone booths. Steel counted the money from his wallet. Had he gone to this pair of shakedown artists with a simple proposition to help Sullivan—had he offered to give them a thousand pounds for doing it— they'd have taken the money and welshed. Or pinched him for attempted bribery. They knew that Sullivan was too hot and that there was nothing that they *could* do. But a safe little shakedown like this was made to their order. What the pair considered the cash value of the inconvenience had been nicely calculated. Twenty pounds against four or five hours in the Hammersmith Police Station.

He handed twenty pounds to York. "What are we supposed to be, *thieves?*" he asked sarcastically.

York pocketed the cash, the broken tooth showing. "I heard you had some of the boys to breakfast the other morning." He shook his head. "Liberty-takers, they are!"

CHAPTER IV

STEEL stood close to the glass of the booth, watching the pair as they went down the steps without looking back. The court attendant was calling silence as Steel found a seat against the wall, close up against the jury box. The judge's bench was just out of sight but he could see the rest of the court. There was a rustle and everybody stood. Followed by a city dignitary in lace ruffles, Judge Croxon bowed his way in, ducking his head first left, then right. He tucked his robes under him and the business of court began.

Slumped in the angle of wall and bench, Steel was thankful that he was not facing the long, grave face. Croxon's thin voice was still as surgical. Three times, he passed sentence on men who were brought up from the cells. He did it dispassionately and without rancour. Steel had the same unwelcome thought that, here, maybe, was a judge without bias or prejudice. Then he remembered what Galt had said about Croxon and crimes involving violence.

Clarke was already in court. Between sentencings, he

bent a bored ear to Galt who fussed from solicitor's table to counsels' bench. Directly underneath the judge, the Clerk to the Court rose and whispered respectfully, almost as if he were in church.

The judge's voice sounded again, brittle but courteous. "You appear for the defence in the next case, Mr. Clarke?"

Clarke came to his feet in sections. When he had the top half of his body in position, he addressed the court. "If it please, m'lord, I was instructed as recently as Friday. There has been very little time to study the brief. In a case as serious as this, I have no hesitation in asking your lordship to stand it over till, say, Tuesday of next week. This is a date convenient to Mr. Trelawney." Defence and prosecuting counsels smiled graciously at one another. There was a whispered consultation between the judge and his clerk. The Croxon's voice, clear and adamant. "No, Mr. Clarke, I think not. This is a case that has been before the court on a previous occasion. It is never fair to either side to allow undue delay. I'm afraid you will have to go on."

"If it please, m'lord." Clarke sat down.

The phrase was beginning to make Steel shift position on his bench. Clarke was strong on respect for tradition, it seemed, but if this were a sample of his aggressiveness, Steel was unimpressed.

A warder's head came to the top of the dock steps, craning to see if the court were ready for his charge. That, thought Steel bitterly, was how you were meant to look innocent. Flanked by jailers in a glass cage. The whole production was calculated to produce but one reaction. "Are you kidding! Why would the guy be there if he hadn't done *something!*"

The jailer snapped his fingers down the steps and Sullivan came up. The long shiv mark showed on his neck, angrily red against the jail pallor.

It was five months since Kosky had slipped from a parked car, a razor in his hand, and sliced into Sullivan from behind. Then, there had been no question of hollering copper. With Sullivan, there couldn't have been. He elected to pay his debts in person.

The Clerk of the Court intoned the indictment with the boredom of habit.

"Daniel George Sullivan. You stand charged upon the indictment with attempted murder. And the particulars state that on the night of 11th August, this year, at the car park belonging to the White City Stadium, you did shoot at with intent to kill one Edward Emanuel Kosky. To that charge, do you plead guilty or not guilty?"

Up came Clarke. "He pleads not guilty, m'lord."

The judge nodded. "Take him below," he instructed the warders. Sullivan disappeared down the steps.

Feet started to shuffle into the jury box above Steel's head. He looked up. Nine men and three women took their places self-consciously. All turned towards the judge as they sat. The Clerk of the Court was on his feet, consulting the roster before him. As each juror answered his name, Steel tried to scribble particulars on a pad. He was the only one in court, apart from officials and a bunch of trainee constables.

Scrawling on the pad, the scheme seemed hopeless. He listened as the Clerk spoke rapidly and the jurors answered. One man's voice cracked with nervousness. A woman dropped the printed card as it was passed to her.

The responses droned on. "I swear by Almight God . . ." ". . . and a true verdict deliver . . ." ". . . according to the evidence . . ."

As soon as each juror had been sworn, the judge's precise voice took command. He inclined his head a little towards the jury box—like some college professor, Steel thought, with infinite patience for an uninstructed audience.

It was a case of attempted murder, said Croxon. Mr. Trelawney appeared for the Crown, Mr. Clarke for the defence. They, the jury, would be sole judges of fact. Croxon permitted himself a thin smile. They would be directed by him in law. Charts, photographs, produced by the Crown were in folders that they would find in front of them. They were to dismiss anything they might have read in the press concerning this case. Their verdict must be based on the evidence that they would hear. It would be a long, possibly a wearying case, but it was their duty to be patient. Finally, they were not to discuss the case other than among themselves.

There was first a sudden hush then a relieved rustle as the judge added: "It is nearly a quarter to one. We will adjourn until five minutes to two."

Steel clambered up, ducking his head. The sense of futility grew. Perhaps it would be better to forget the cloak and dagger stuff. Sullivan had the best legal help in the city. If once the wrong juror were approached—someone who would go through the motions of listening with sympathy and then set a trap—it would be disastrous. Even if Steel were able to avoid a pinch, nobody would believe that Sullivan had been innocent of an attempt to fix the jury.

He made his way down to the incongruously modern cafeteria and queued with junior cops, still living on their pay, minor court officials and a few solicitors' clerks. He carried the coffee and sandwich to a corner table. To the left, a corridor led to the jailer's office. Beyond that was the network of corridors and cells where the prisoners were locked up. The memory of the tiny steel boxes was sharp in Steel's mind.

With him, hope and despair were opposing ends of a

55

seesaw that tipped violently and often for no apparent reason. Ambivalence, the psychiatrists called it. Now he was suddenly confident again. In England, you had a job convincing the man in the street that a cop could be dishonest. To the average citizen, a cop was a symbol of justice, copper-plated and untarnishable. If you tried to peddle the same guy the idea that a juror could be approached and bribed—bullied—pleaded with—your listener would have you pegged as a bar-room bore. A loudmouth with a taste for the sensational. When it came to the cops, the public had its giraffe head in pink clouds and refused to see what was going on between its legs.

He sipped the grey coffee and looked at the list he had made. Names were scrawled so hurriedly that they ran into one another. He was able to decipher—Cluett, Felton, Bevan. Three names that he could fit to faces. One of them, he would have to follow home. He was uncertain whether a juror had a police escort in England. One thing was sure. Either all twelve would have someone breathing heavily down their necks all the way home or none.

By the time the court adjourned that night, the light would be failing. It would be no trick to ascertain whether a juror had a police tail. If they *were* escorted, it made his job that much rougher. The prospect of pulling one of the twelve on the steps of the Central Criminal Court was impressive but disturbing. He had no time to waste playing bird-dog yet in this he had to be certain.

Last time, the case had gone four days and here he was, Tuesday. Come Friday night, the jury might be yawning its way to a verdict. Before then, he had to have one of them in his pocket. He pushed the cup away, leaving the ungenerous sandwich half-eaten. Your mind worked in an odd way. In jail in Canada, there'd been a battery of

56

tests. I.Q. Tests, Achievements Tests, the weird performance when the bug doctor shoved pictures of inkblots
under your nose and recorded your impressions. One blot
had looked like a Christmas tree—an answer that drew
a grin from the young psychologist. "You're cheating,
Mack," he'd said. Then Steel had understood. To a
psychopath, the blot wasn't *meant* to look like a Christmas
tree but a phallic symbol. Then there'd been word-
association. "Black," the man said. "Chimney," you
answered. "Sky"—"Blue." "Woman"—"Trouble." Now
when the word "verdict" came into his head, he thought
"guilty."

He shut his eyes for a moment, content not to think but
to let his mind loaf till the night and the darkness. The
crackling Public Address system pulled him back to
reality, pageing a court official. The clock said almost
two. Steel hurried up the stairs. In the lobby, he passed
York and the other cop. They looked through him,
making their eyes blank.

Galt had already gone into court but Sheila was
waiting. The public benches were almost full. The same
bunch of rookie cops sat, pencils and papers ready. In
the benches reserved for friends of City officials, two
women sat wearing mink and feather hats. Behind Clarke
and Trelawney was a group of young barristers, self-
conscious in their new, powder-grey wigs. The cop on
the door made room for Steel and Sheila on a bench
behind the dock. On their heels, York and his partner
went to their places, beefily righteous.

Once again, the usher's bawl brought the court to its
feet as the small, scarlet robed figure came in. With
Croxon's second bow, everyone sat. The jurors answered
their names with more assurance now. Steel kept his eye
on them. Hilda Cluett was on his list—an obvious spinster
with a thin mouth and an eager way of answering—as

if she were anxious to get down to business. Steel mentally thumbed down all women on the jury. This reduced his names to two—Bevan and Felton. Bevan was the foreman, highdomed and with a solemn manner. A foreman was tempting but Steel let him out—nothing would overrule the glory of Bevan's Great Day.

Felton sat on the front row of the jury, immediately over Steel's head. He was broad-shouldered and fair— about Steel's age. His dull blue tie, white shirt and grey suit were worn as if the juror cared about such things. He wore a flower in his lapel and was busy doodling on the pad in front of him. Compared to Felton, the other jurors were yokels.

The Treasury counsel sipped water and glanced at the papers that were on a portable stand. Shortly, he outlined the case for the prosecution and called his first witness.

York took the stand and swore his truthful intention with practised ease. He was a Detective-Inspector, attached to the Flying Squad, New Scotland Yard. At 2 a.m., 12th August of this year, in company with other officers and as a result of what he had heard, he went to premises in Grove Road, Chiswick. There he saw the defendant, Daniel Sullivan. He told Sullivan that he had a warrant of arrest on a charge of attempted murder, that he proposed to take Sullivan to Hammersmith Police Station.

York lowered his red face into the note-book in front of him. It was a rendition of the police officer being scrupulously fair to the point of embarrassment.

"Sullivan said, sir, 'Who—me? I haven't been out of the house all the evening. It's about time you —— coppers left me alone'." The detective cleared his throat. "In company with other officers, I took Sullivan to Hammersmith Police Station where I cautioned, then charged him.

He replied . . ." again, York wet a heavy finger and flipped a couple of pages in the note-book. "He replied, 'I'll say nothing till I've seen my lawyer. Is Kosky hurt bad?' "

His head between his hands, Steel sneaked a look at the jury. Most of them were swivelling attention from detective to Crown counsel, heads moving as answer followed question. Felton, his elegant grey-flannelled shoulders fitted snugly into his chair back, seemed more interested in the defendant than in the evidence.

York went on. In company with other officers he returned to the Sullivan house with a search warrant. He did, in fact, search that house but took nothing away. Subsequently, he went to several business premises owned by the prisoner and searched them. On that occasion, he removed certain papers which had since been returned to the defendant's solicitor. With the end of his tale, York gazed at the ceiling. York's examination-in-chief was over.

Clarke uncranked his great length. He spoke to York but faced the jury as if compelling them to attention.

"Officer," he said pleasantly. "You say that you went in company with other officers to Mr. Sullivan's home at two o'clock in the morning. Isn't it a fact that when you arrived, you both rang and knocked for some time before being admitted?"

"That is right." The detective was completely at ease.

"The first sign that anyone in that house heard this din was when Mr. Sullivan himself appeared at his bedroom window, wasn't it? He asked you what you wanted?" York mumbled something. "Speak up," instructed Clarke, "we all want to be able to hear what you say. And please watch me, not Mr. Trelawney."

"The prisoner leaned out of the window and shouted," York gave the words as much injury as he could.

Clarke nodded. "He said 'What's going on, down

59

there!' or something like it, did he not? Yes. At any rate, you told him you were police officers and then he came down and let you in. I believe, York, that on occasions like this, you sometimes surround the house? Had you done so on this night?"

York hesitated. "Acting on instructions . . ." he began.

"Well, had you?"

"No," answered York.

"Then, presumably, Mr. Sullivan was in his bed—like most people at that hour—asleep. He hears this noise outside, asks you what you want and when he hears that you're policemen, comes down and lets you into his house."

"I had a warrant."

"I know." Clarke leaned back, lifting a foot to the bench. "But presumably, you didn't shout out 'We are police with a warrant for your arrest!' did you? Not at two in the morning!"

"I told him I had a warrant," York said doggedly.

"Very well. And then he came down to let you in. How was he dressed?"

"In his pyjamas."

Clarke smiled. "It's understandable. From when you first arrived at Grove Road till the time Mr. Sullivan opened the front door would be about how long, officer?"

The red face panned to the ceiling again. "About ten—twelve minutes, sir."

"So that there were ten or twelve minutes in which Mr. Sullivan might have been clambering over his back garden wall had he wished?"

"If he'd heard us at first, yes."

"But *you* tell us that you shouted up that you had a search warrant for his arrest. Certainly, then, he might have escaped. Remember, officer, you had been ringing on doorbells, battering the door, We shall hear that not

60

only did you wake Mr. Sullivan but his wife, his child and the maid."

York moved his tongue across his lips. "He didn't come down, not for ten minutes."

Clarke's wave justified the picture of an innocent man suddenly awakened, failing to spring from his bed and answer the door. "Just one more question, officer. You have told my lord and the jury that when he was charged, Sullivan said—" the lawyer glanced down at his notes. " 'I'll say nothing till I've seen my lawyer. Is Kosky hurt bad?' Now part of your caution to him had been to the effect that he was *not* obliged to make any statement in answer to the charge. Isn't that right?"

"That's right, sir."

"And, of course, since he had been charged, he knew the name of the man he was alleged to have assaulted was Kosky? Officer," asked Clarke, "have you personal knowledge whether these two men were acquainted before the night of 11th August?"

Here York regained confidence. He drew a deep breath. "I have. As long ago as ten years, I had them under observation at the same time."

Clarke lifted his foot from the bench. He spoke quietly. "You told us that you have been twenty years on the Metropolitan Police Force. You know perfectly well that was a highly improper way of answering." He glanced at the judge. The scarlet-gowned figure leaned over.

"Don't elaborate, officer. Are you saying that as long as ten years ago, to your certain knowledge, these two men were acquainted? Never mind why or how."

"They were, sir. I do, my lord."

Clarke was not done. "So that Mr. Sullivan's remark, 'Is Kosky hurt bad?' is really a natural enquiry about someone he has known for ten years?"

"If you put it like that, sir."

Clarke started down to his seat. "That's how I do put it, York. It's not quite the same as the way you put it. No more questions."

The afternoon wore on. One after another, the technical experts took the stand. Police photographers proved the authenticity of pictures produced as exhibits. A ballistics specialist swore that he had examined the shells found in the roof of a car. They were from a 45 mm. automatic pistol.

Last witness of the afternoon was a doctor on duty in the Casualty Ward of Hammersmith Hospital on the night of 11th August. He had treated Edward Kosky for a superficial head wound, one inch below the hair line. The wound was such as might have been caused by a shot from a pistol described by the previous witness.

It was four-thirty by Steel's watch with the sky darkening through the high windows. The judge adjourned for the day. As they took Sullivan below Sheila's black-gloved fingers waved mute greeting. With the judge gone, the jury sat for a moment, chatting together. Clarke yawned, and reaching across Trelawney, pointed at a page in the brief. Both men laughed. The police were packing their papers.

There was no time to grope for an excuse. "Listen, Sheila," Steel said. "I've got to go somewhere. I'll call you later to-night." He patted her arm and pushed his way from the court.

CHAPTER V

HE unlocked the Zephyr and wiped the inside of the windshield with the heel of his gloved hand. It was not certain that the jury would leave by the same exit that he had used. But hanging around in the court-room or the entrance hall would create a risk of becoming involved with Sheila. Worse—of attracting the attention of York and his partner.

This guy Felton was tall. The grey suit and stone-coloured top-coat easy to spot. There was a steady bustle down the steps by now. York, who waved to a squad car which drew up alongside. Then Sheila. Steel slid down in his seat till his shoulder blades were almost on the cushion. Eyes aloof, she passed within feet of the car.

Further down, where the street narrowed, the big doors were opening. A uniformed constable stopped the traffic and the Brixton coach rolled out. Though the coach was lighted, Steel could not see Sullivan. The vehicle moved south with none of the passers-by giving it a second glance.

Steel knew every inch of that route, from the Old Bailey till it struck across the desolate waste of Clapham Common. Twice on that journey across the common, the coach was bound to slow almost to a halt. At either moment, a determined man with a hammer could shatter the glass from the outside—an alerted prisoner might dive through the hole to a waiting car. And then what! Every cop and police informer in the country on Sullivan's tail. It wasn't the answer.

63

He bent forward, squinting through the glass at the steps. Sour with sudden futility, he had mockery for his role. Scarlet Pimpernel, he gibed. Steel—the hope of the damned. These past three years with their freedom from fear had turned him soft. He'd earned good money, broken no laws and slept as easily as his digestion allowed. But without Sullivan, there *was* no job. He'd be back where he was, three years ago, on this very street. Better take one chance than go back to taking them every day. Honesty was less a matter of ethics than self-interest.

His breath had steamed the windshield. He rubbed furiously at it. Between the double doors at the top of the steps, Felton had stopped to light a cigarette. Ignoring two of his colleagues who passed, the juryman left the court building and turned to the right.

Steel opened the door of the car cautiously. Felton turned the corner and walked east towards the city. Ducking his head into the wind, Steel followed. Nobody like a cop was in sight. Felton's light coat was a marker ahead. The juror seemed to be making for the Underground station, a couple of hundred yards in front of him. Nearby, a cab slowed. Steel hesitated long enough for the figure ahead to disappear. Steel forced himself to a run, fighting his whipping coat. On the right a narrow street cut down to Cheapside, passing the bomb site used as a car park. There was no doorway Felton might have used. Steel trotted down the intersection. As he passed the hut at the car park entrance a Vauxhall swung out, one fender brushing him. Felton was at the wheel, alone in the car.

A stitch doubled Steel. He bent his body, gasping. Then walking slowly he went back to his car. Irresolute, he sat at the wheel. He had been right. For this jury, there was neither police surveillance nor escort. Felton's address was one of the three on the paper in his pocket.

Markham Square, Chelsea. No more than a couple of hundred yards from Steel's rooms.

He juggled the pennies in his hand. Ten past five. Alan should be home by now. Before tomorrow morning, Steel had to find out as much as he could about Felton. He already knew where the juror lived—he must know *how* the man lived. The Chelsea Public Library stayed open till nine. Reference books might help or, maybe Felton used a pub in the neighbourhood—some place where he might be picked up over a glass of scotch. People talked in pubs.

He walked over to the 'phone booth by the lavatories. With any luck, Sheila wouldn't have reached Chiswick. He dialled Sullivan's number. Alan answered.

Steel made it short. "Is Sheila back? Well, get out before she is. Meet me at six at the Chelsea Library. That's Manresa Road. If I'm not in the car, it'll be parked outside, unlocked. Get in and wait."

"All right," said Alan. The line went dead.

Steel drove fast, cutting over to the south bank of the river to avoid the traffic. At the power station, he headed north again and filtered into the King's Road. Outside the library steps, he parked and went upstairs. Grabbing an armful of reference books, he went to the counter. Each library had a copy of the voters' list for the borough. A girl brought it. He scanned Burke's, Who's Who, the Directory of Directors. There was no mention of Felton. To go through every directory would take more time than he had. He already knew the number of Felton's house. It was one of a group of conversions on the north side of the square, replacing the paint-peeled originals. There'd be no change from ten thousand pounds for a house like that. Just how much did you offer the man who lived there! What kind of money would outweigh his conscience! Steel had control of Sullivan's business accounts.

The case had put a crimp in the balance but there was still enough to put a thousand pounds on this guy's table— if it was money that would move him. But no more.

He looked up, in the green-shaded light, at the depressed library assistants—the quiet earnest faces of the men across the table wondering which of them wouldn't take a thousand pounds to say "Not guilty". And *keep* saying it till the judge sent them home in disgust. No—the thing that kept people honest was the fear of the consequences. Felton had to be more than moved. He had to be convinced that whatever he did would involve him in no danger.

Steel closed the directories. He still knew no more about Clive Felton than a six-months-old voters' list told him. According to it, only one person lived at the Markham Square address. Felton. Well—at least there'd be no woman acting as keeper of the man's conscience.

As he went downstairs and out to the car, it was six by the library clock. He sat in the car and waited. A cab coming from the direction of Chelsea Square stopped in front of him. In the light from the street lamp, he could see Alan paying off the driver. There was no question of telling the kid what to do—Steel didn't know himself. He swung the door of the Zephyr open and ready.

Alan climbed in, tense with the effort of showing indifference. To ease him, Steel talked for ten minutes with half-felt conviction. Then he flipped the *Gauloise* stub through the window. "Let's get going," he said. "We'll take a look at the house, first. Then we'll separate. I'll cover the pubs round about—you take the espresso bars along the King's Road." He turned his head so that he could see the younger man. "You still feel all right about things?"

Alan wound up the window. "I'll feel better if you don't keep talking about it."

Steel wheeled the car into the King's Road traffic. He talked as he drove. "Don't go in asking if they know a Mr. Felton. Just ask if Felton's been in to-night. If they don't know him, get out. But if someone says 'That's him over there,' you say 'Wrong guy' and come back and report. O.K.?"

Alan nodded, trying to look as if the advice were wasted.

They drove towards Sloane Square for three hundred yards then north into Markham Square. An iron fence enclosed the centre garden. Trees and shrubbery were dark and wet. Steel edged the car to the top of the square. In the corner a standard threw a segment of light that he avoided, parking under the trees. In front of him was a half-dozen of the converted modern houses, a great deal of glass and wrought iron. Felton's was the end one, facing due south. The hall was lit. Badly-drawn curtains showed a light in the room to the left of the front door. Felton's Vauxhall was parked in front.

"Now what?" whispered Alan.

This was typical, Steel thought with sudden distaste. From having wet pants, Alan was a kid at a party, waiting for the conjuror to produce a rabbit from every hat. Without answering, he opened the Zephyr door and walked across to Felton's car. Back to the door, he looked at the sky while his hands tried the handle. It was locked.

Another car turned into the square from the King's Road, lighting the road. Before it reached the turn, he was back in the shelter of the Zephyr. It was a cab that stopped in front of Felton's house. A woman got out.

She was tall and the high thin heels on her shoes accentuated her height. Long hair swung unfashionably as she leaned into the cab, paying the driver. Watching the house, Steel saw the curtains move, then the front door opened. The woman passed into the patch of light as the door closed. No sign, no greeting was given by the woman or Felton.

In the car, the two men sat shoulder to shoulder. There was a nervous laugh, then Alan said it again—"Now what?"

For Steel, it was the end of a long day. The stink of jail, the leering face of York—had left no room for tolerance in him. Alan shifted to a sprawl, his legs crossed comfortably, fingers drumming idly on the dash.

Steel swung his arm, slamming the other's fingers against the dashboard. Then Steel had him by the coat collar, holding him with a shaking hand. They sat in the dark like that till Alan moved his body in pain. His voice cracked. "Gerry!" He twisted. "Let me go, Gerry."

Steel's stomach was sick. "Just stop asking that goddam question," he whispered. "Stop it. Do you understand?"

As the street door opened again, they dug into the floorboards with their feet. Felton and the woman stood in the hallway, their shadows long in the light that reached to the radiator of the parked Zephyr. Both men slid lower in their seats. The house door closed and Felton and the woman came past his own car, heading for the King's Road.

When they were past Steel jerked the door of the Zephyr. "If they keep walking, stay on their tail till they're settled. But if they grab a cab or something, come right back here." He half-shoved, half-patted Alan to the road. He watched as the younger man walked south. In that quiet stretch it was not easy to follow unobtrusively. Eager now, Alan kept twenty yards behind the others. Then all three turned right into the King's Road.

The light still burned in the hall. There was no sign of life anywhere else in Felton's house. Steel opened the car door cautiously. He got out and stood for a second, listening. A dog barked, far away. Further down, a noisy drink party was going on. Behind it all was the sound of the traffic from the highway. He let the door swing under its own weight, easing it so that the lock did not shoot home. In a hurry, a jerk would open it. He walked over to the wrought-iron gate and lifted the latch with gloved fingers. At the street door he pulled a cigarette from the pack and bent his head to the lighter flame. The two locks on the door were an Ingersoll and a Hobbs mortise. To beat either, he needed better tools than the rubbish under the car carpet. To the left of the door, a bow window made an arc to the dividing wall. Beyond the glass, there, something moved. Inside the room, the curtains were swinging lightly in the current of air. A window had been left open.

The sound of someone walking came from behind Steel. Exaggerating his movements, like an actor in mime, he glanced at his watch, the door, then shrugged. He closed the gate behind him and walked away from his car, towards the oncomer. It was Alan. They turned and walked to the parked Zephyr.

"They're in that Chinese restaurant, round the corner." Alan was breathing hard as though he had been running. "I went in after them and booked a table for four. He was just ordering as I left." As if apprehensive of Steel's silence, he finished—"was that right?"

"Sure. You did fine." Steel tried to keep the impatience from his voice. "They should be good for a half-hour, at the very least. More, with any luck."

The house was empty. The window should give him no trouble. He had to take a chance if the place was belled. Felton's home would provide more answers than a hundred reference books. There would be personal papers. It was possible that the juror had made notes that afternoon. Steel would be in and out in a quarter-hour. He made his decision.

"You wait in the car, Alan. Back it up twenty yards nearer the King's Road and *keep your eye on that corner*! If you see them coming before I'm out, sound the horn twice. Then take the car round to the Admiral Codrington. Wait there fifteen minutes. If I don't show, leave the car outside my place and go home. O.K.?" Alan nodded and Steel passed him the car keys, moving over to let the other in behind the wheel.

"What are you going . . ." Alan started. He left the question unfinished. In his embarrassment, he leaned on the horn. A strident blast echoed in the square.

"Christ!" Steel said sharply. "You clumsy bastard." They waited for a moment but the sound of the horn passed unnoticed.

Steel wasted no more time. As he reached Felton's street door, Alan was reversing the Zephyr. The kid wasn't too bad, he thought with approval. Now the Zephyr faced the King's Road. His hand went through the open window. The screw on the bar was stiff. He was beginning to sweat. He stood on his toes for more leverage and twisted. Under cover of the passing Zephyr, he jumped up on the sill and let himself into the room.

He stood for a while in the darkness, completely immobile, while his senses got the feel of the house. The room was warm and smelt of a woman's scent. A clock ticked softly to his right. Gradually, his eyes gave shape to the furniture, the fireplace. There was no danger that his crêpe-soled shoes would leave prints. He was treading on a deep pile carpet. He pulled the window shut and opened the door to the hall. A writing desk showed in the half-light, littered with papers. In the far corner of the room was a small grand piano. On the other wall, a bookcase, its base at knee-level. The room was peaceful and lived-in.

He shut the door after him and went to the back of the house, avoiding the polished boards. Downstairs were a kitchen and pantry, a closed door that he opened with care. A pair of binoculars hung from a hook, festooned with member's badges. On a table by the wash-basin, a pile of old *New Yorkers*. If Felton were a betting man, it might make things easier.

Steel ran up the stairs. At the half-landing, a wall heater glowed over an old Spanish chest. On the second floor, there was light enough from the hall for him to see. The house was small with only two bedrooms. In the front room, overlooking the square, there were two beds but the covers were down on one only. The other bedroom was unoccupied. He moved more surely now, obeying familiar rules without thinking. First, he had to find an escape route from the house. Page one in the burglar's manual, he remembered. Unconsciously, he was whistling softly through his teeth as he had done in the old days. He went down the stairs again and explored the kitchen. The back door led to a small flagged court with a striped parasol and gaily-painted table, incongruous in the raw night. At the end of the tiny courtyard, a wall higher than his head allowed access to the backs of the houses behind. Unless in the worst kind of trouble, there was no way out there. He shut the door and went back to the hall. He had to work fast. The papers in the drawing-room, maybe. No, first the bedroom. There would be suits with tailor's labels. He might hit pay-dirt in the dressingtable drawers. After all this time and here he was back at the old stand! But with a new kind of burglary. He was going to walk out of the place without so much as a kitchen spoon belonging to the juryman. But tomorrow was different. This was as far as Felton's luck took him. Tomorrow Steel would bribe, bluff or blackmail, whichever seemed best.

He was half-way up the stairs when the horn sounded twice in the square. He ran down and stood at the drawn curtains. The Zephyr rounded the bend, slowly. As it passed the house, the horn bleated again, softly. Steel could hear footsteps on the paving stones. Felton and the woman came into view, walking towards the house. They were no more than twenty yards away. If Steel went through the window or door at the front, he would land in their arms.

It took seconds to ensure that he had left no trace of his entry downstairs. He took the stairs, three at a time. On the second floor, he transferred the key of the unused bedroom to the inside and stood with the door slightly open. He waited.

Downstairs, things started happening quickly. The street door opened and shut with a crash. Then came the woman's voice, edged with alcohol. "No scenes!" she parodied. "You're always so bloody concerned with appearances, aren't you!" Glass chinked and Steel heard the splash of a soda siphon. Both Felton and the woman had gone through to the drawing-room.

Steel opened the bedroom door an inch at a time. Beyond the half-landing he could see a patch of the hall. The woman's coat was on the floor next to her handbag. Felton's voice answered, not over-patient. "Even when you're sober, Anne, I get tired of your abuse. When you're drunk, it's both vulgar and offensive. In either case, I no longer have to take it—especially in front of an audience of waiters."

"You don't!" The laugh merged with a hiccough. "You don't!" she repeated as if the sense of the words had been forgotten. The rest came with a rush. "*I* don't care *where* I tell you the truth. If you'd sooner listen to it here, so much the better! I've had eighteen months freedom

72

from the great creative artist—the genius who had to have his freedom. And what am I supposed to be—heart-broken?" She laughed again. "I've only had my own bills to pay." She was shouting now. "Freedom! You've had it, and, by God, I've been well rid of you!"

In the silence that followed, Steel moved softly to the edge of the banister and into the shadow of the alcove. Through the half-open door to the drawing-room, he saw Felton's legs as they crossed the room. Then he heard the sound of the window being shut.

"Charming," said Felton. "The neighbours will be enjoying it. At any rate, we both seem to have got what we wanted. I don't understand what your complaint is. 'I don't want a penny of your money, Clive,' that's what you said. All right—you're a wealthy woman—you can afford the luxury. We were to lead our own lives. We did that, too." The grey-flannelled legs recrossed the strip of light. "You must have forgotten that seeing you to-day wasn't my idea in the first place. A sensible talk over lunch, you said. With no unpleasantness, no scenes." His laugh was a bark. "I knew *that* would be too good to be true."

"A cigarette," she said mechanically. "I want a cigarette."

There was movement in the hall. Steel barely had time to get back to the wall—heels and the palms of his hands pressed tightly against it. Felton's wife swayed over her coat, fumbling at the pockets. She found cigarettes and let the coat fall back to the floor.

She went back to the drawing-room. Her voice attacked again. "Lunch on Monday with Clive," she recited, "one-fifteen at Hatchett's. Do you know how long I sat there—from one-fifteen till three!"

"In the bar presumably," Felton said drily.

"In-the-bloody-bar!" she answered. "Simply because

73

you hadn't the manners to 'phone." Her voice rose again.
"You could always fool other people with that phoney
gallantry. 'So charming, your husband! Such perfect
manners!'" She laughed till she forgot what she was
laughing at. "Manners of a pig," she said viciously.

Felton's was the flat recital of a tale told many times
but unaccepted. "I wrote on Friday saying that I'd been
called for this Old Bailey business. I hadn't any idea that
you wouldn't be back from the country. That you were
away, even."

"Posserby." She corrected herself with drunken dignity
—"Possibly, what I do at the weekend is no longer any
concern of yours. None whatsoever. Two hours in a bar,"
she complained. "Surrounded by bores trying to pick
you up. Because of a husband with the manners of
a pig."

"You'd better forget it for to-night, Anne," Felton
said suddenly. "I'll call you tomorrow. I've explained a
dozen times but obviously it isn't going to do any good.
You just don't *do* as you like when you're sitting on a
jury."

For a moment, the three in the house waited in the
silence. The house had sounds of its own. The refrigerator
whirred in the kitchen. A tread in the stairway decided
to move. Instinctively, Steel tensed for what was coming.
There was the sound of breaking glass as though something had been hurled across the room. Then the laughter
cracking as Felton's wife lost her breath.

"Christ! How ridiculous it all is! This bloody picture
of the outstanding citizen sitting in judgment on some
poor devil unlucky enough to have been caught."

"Shut up!" There was the flat unmistakeable sound of a
palm meeting flesh.

The woman's voice was quiet again now. Sobered and
bitter. "Of course," she said. "That's all it wanted.

A gentleman and a juryman. You bastard," she said slowly. "You know, Clive, things I remember, you choose to forget. That's one of the reasons I wanted to see you to-day. To tell you the income tax people have been asking me questions about you. Remember, Rome twice and Paris. The three scripts you did for Fichtler. They paid you in francs and in lira and you never declared a penny." As she came through into the hall, Steel backed into the empty room and closed the door to a slit.

She leaned over wearily and picked up her coat. "I want you to remember something else when you remember to-night, Clive. I was with you in Paris and in Rome. Every stinking rotten lonely night of it, I was there. The daytimes were better. The creative urge didn't bother you until cocktail time. I was with you during the day, wasn't I, Clive? I haven't forgotten. I can remember who paid you, where and exactly how much." She opened the front door. "Good night, Clive."

She went out into the quiet square, trailing her coat by the loop in the collar. She never turned her head. Not until she was out of sight did Felton close the door.

For a long time, the two men stood there without moving. Through the crack in the bedroom door, Steel saw Felton's foreshortened shoulders less chipper. Less elegant. The juryman's hand moved uncertainly to his head then to his face. He went into the drawing-room. Steel heard the sound of glass being collected into a pan, then Felton went through to the kitchen.

Success depended on a finesse play. This was an unused room. Three hundred and sixty-five days a year, you could bet that Felton climbed the stairs, went to his own room and the bathroom, then to bed. There was nothing here he could want. Quietly, Steel pushed the door and turned the key. If that door handle moved, he would go through the window and take a chance with the wall, the

75

gardens beyond. If not, as soon as Felton slept, he would go out the sensible way. Through the front door.

No sound came from below. He needed a cigarette the worst way but dare not risk the distinctive smell of the strong French tobacco. He sat in the hard chair by the open window, his eyes on the door.

Anne Felton's last words to her husband were still clear in Steel's mind. Her tone—Felton's reaction—suggested that she was telling the truth. And if Felton was a tax-dodger, he couldn't have a better prospect. There was no pity in Steel for the man below. That was a sentiment reserved for a crippled dog, a hunted fox. People were either for or against you. Your friends needed help, not pity. Your enemies the axe. Till he was a friend, the juror was an enemy. It was as simple as that.

He leaned forward in the chair as a bright strip of light showed suddenly at the bottom of the door. The blue carpet on the inside was plain. There was a cough as Felton passed the door and went into his bedroom. Then came the sound of running water, the wet, sweet smell of a bathroom being used. After a while, the button was flipped on the landing and the light went out at the foot of the door.

It was completely dark in the bedroom. Only by lifting his wrist to the window could Steel see the time. A quarter to ten. He walked on his toes to the wall between the two rooms and put his ear against it. He could hear nothing.

For an hour, he sat in the chair, as relaxed now as if the house were his own. It was almost eleven when he eased himself to his feet. Leaving the window open, he walked to the door. Warped wood had given it the smallest drop so that tongue and lock were not perfectly true. He lifted the box of the lock slightly. Holding it so that there would be no strain, he turned the key gently. Then the door handle, pulling the door open gradually.

He could smell the warmth of the hall and the landing. Both were in darkness. The door to Felton's bedroom was shut. Steel made one last trip to lower and bolt the window then went back to the landing.

He took the stairs slowly, letting the wood of each tread settle under his weight before he moved down to the next. The clock in the drawing-room ticked softly. He felt his way towards the sound. In spite of the window that had been left ajar, the stale smell of smoke and liquor hung heavy in there. In the short time he had spent in the room earlier, he had noticed a book by the telephone. He groped his way past the piano till his fingers touched the leather binding. Then he snapped his lighter. In its flame, he searched the A's till he found what he wanted.

ANNE—there was an address off Regent's Park and a telephone number. Steel copied both to a piece of paper.

The curtains were back. He stood at the window, alert for a movement from the outside. Beyond the dark, broken outline of the trees in the square, the last buses rattled their way along the King's Road. Further away, voices were bawling discordant with drink. With even greater care, he scanned the railings, the steps to the basements. In these quiet squares, a cop on patrol often holed up in a basement area for a smoke. But the square seemed to be sleeping. Steadying himself with one hand, he lowered his legs through the window. He turned and polished the painted ledge with his handkerchief. The iron gate swung easily and he was on the sidewalk. Briefly, he looked up at Felton's window. Nothing moved.

In spite of the chill in the night, he walked back to Draycott Place feeling warm. The familiar shape of the Zephyr was in front of his house. Alan had left the car unlocked, the keys were on top of the sun visor. Steel pocketed them and went into the silent house. Hunger had come then gone. He ate a banana and read at the

77

afternoon papers. Now that Sullivan's case was being heard, the journalists had gone back to dead-pan reporting of the day's proceedings. At the time of the first trial, the public had been given the entire story with banner headlines. Only the end had been unwritten. As far as the press was concerned, there would be a choice of two headlines when the jury came back, this time. It would be either"—Gangster Convicted"—or—"Car Dealer Freed". The verdict made a great deal of difference to the way they would describe Sullivan.

He lay for a long while in the high-ceilinged room. Some of the fear had gone to be replaced with the old sense of power. The private knowledge of another man's home—his hopes, his secrets. Felton, after all, was no different to anyone else. There wasn't a single man or woman on that jury who hadn't *something* to hide. A hunch and a drunken woman had tossed Felton to him without a struggle.

He twisted in his bed, reaching for a last cigarette. Felton was his meat—whether by bribe or by threat. The sooner the first move was made, the better. Tomorrow, after Felton had left the court was the obvious time to tackle the juror. How—he stubbed out the butt and pulled up the covers—there were twenty hours to think up an answer. He slept soundly without dreaming.

CHAPTER VI

WEDNESDAY was bright with a pale October sun. He called Alan from a booth on Sloane Square. Sheila answered.

Steel's impatience with her carefully controlled curiosity was growing.

"Just get Alan," he said quietly. "I'm at Sloane Square and I've still got to have breakfast before I go to court."

Alan's voice was guarded. Steel guessed that the girl was still by the 'phone. "Bring those pictures to the Old Bailey," he instructed. "I'll wait in the car park behind the court. Four-thirty. And see you're on time."

He stood where he was for a while, indifferent to the man outside who glanced at his watch pointedly. If Sheila ever found out what was going on, she'd do her best to scotch the scheme. Her idea of what was best for her husband was part of her background. And of her sex. She reasoned that since Sullivan was already in trouble it would be wrong to run the risk of involving him still deeper. Steel took the same circumstances and came up with a different conclusion. The kind of trouble Sullivan was in justified *any* means employed to get him out.

He opened the door to the booth. Testy with impatience, the man waiting gave him a sour look of disapproval. "If you've got nothing to do but daydream, it's a pity you can't find somewhere else to do it." The man pushed by him.

It was twenty past ten when he turned the Zephyr into the car park behind the Central Criminal Court. Felton's Vauxhall was already by the side of the entrance. Three cars away was a space into which Steel manoeuvred the Zephyr. Then, he walked round to the front of the court.

The congregation of witnesses waiting upstairs had a few stragglers at the head of the wide stairway. To reach Sheila and Galt on the far side, Steel was obliged to pass a group, including York and Kosky. Kosky, the star prosecution witness. With that rag round his head, Steel sneered, trying to look like some goddam wounded hero.

Sheila wore the same dark suit as on the previous day. And still played with her marriage ring, he noted sourly. As if it were some talisman that would save her happiness. Playing Sister Anne instead of worrying how to get Sullivan out of jail and into his home.

Steel's good morning to Sheila and the lawyer was an offhand nod. Galt's eyes fussed from his watch to the clock on the wall. "Not so good, Gerry," he said. Steel had an irrational pleasure at the lawyer's concern—some of the bounce and pomp had gone. "They've served copies of additional evidence," Galt added.

Steel took a quick glance at Sheila's pallor. The texture of her skin was waxen and her mouth bloodless. She stood there without a word as if she neither knew nor cared what they were talking about. Resigned to doom, death and disaster.

"Additional evidence?" Steel answered. "What of it?"

There were people standing near and Galt kept his voice low. "I warned you. It's always the way when there's been a previous trial. The Crown gets the chance to plug leaks. Apart from Kosky's evidence the testimony at the first trial was circumstantial. And Kosky was no real corroboration. The pistol . . ." he said hesitantly.

"What *about* the goddam pistol?" asked Steel. "No-one's ever produced a gun—still less tied it to Sullivan!"

Galt let his annoyance show. "I wish you'd drop this aggressive attitude. I know the value of evidence without you telling me. Taken singly, not one factor is worthy of consideration. Without corroboration, a jury might think Kosky's story to be straight lying. This new evidence complicates matters. The Crown is producing a witness who will say that he saw Sullivan with a gun in his hand—saw him fire at Kosky."

"How comes it that you only hear about it now?" Mistrust sent the blood to Steel's face, twisted his mouth.

The new complication didn't really matter; with a juror tied up. But this fat bum had been paid a lot of money. Steel fixed on the bland round face, searching for some confession of incompetence.

Now Galt was giving as much as he got. "Because, my friend, contrary to your obvious opinion, it happens that I'm not acting for the Crown. They don't tell me these things till it suits them."

Sheila's voice was brusque and sudden. "I wanted to say this before, Gerry. I know Danny has complete confidence in Mr. Galt—I wish you'd let him do what's necessary without . . ."

"Without interfering?" Steel grinned. The two of them were useless. Sheila with this wide-eyed belief in crap like "Own up the boy who did that!"—"Out of evil cometh good"! Then this smooth phoney who was probably already preparing excuses against the time when he had to admit failure. Well, once Sullivan was free, Steel would have fun letting the pair of them know just how he had felt, standing there listening to their crap. Snug in the secret certainty, he shrugged. "Anything you say, Sheila. Mr. Galt knows what's best and Mr. Galt has my apologies."

The lawyer's plump hand waved acceptance. "I'll have information about this new witness before the morning's over. Clarke may bring out things about your husband's record," he warned Sheila. "If he does, don't be alarmed—this case is a long way from being lost."

The hands of the clock hurried them into the court. The two seats on the bench behind the dock were free and they took them. The warders brought Sullivan up from below. As he reached the top of the steps, he looked down where they sat but his look was for Sheila. In that brief moment, the square lined face was without evil, the Code forgotten. Need not bravado showed in his eyes. And in

Sheila's, love. Sullivan turned his back. The scar showed, a sinister badge of defiance.

Steel angled his head to see past the corner of the dock. Though it was only the second day of the trial, some of the jury were showing peculiarities that distinguished them from the rest. Hilda Cluett next to the foreman, thin-lipped and bird-bright with interest, tapping bony fingers on her neighbour's folder of photographs. The tall man in the back row, who sat bolt upright, his arms folded across his chest and his eyes shut tight. And Felton.

Felton was in the same seat. In the front row, at the end nearest the dock. He was rotating a pencil slowly between finger and thumb. As the first witness of the day was called, he turned his head idly towards Sullivan.

A script-writer, his wife had said, Steel remembered. Busy looking for material, possibly. Before the day was over, he'd have plenty.

"Mark Adler," called Trelawney.

A dark little man was herded into the witness box. He stood there, blinking apologetically behind thick-framed glasses. He consulted the usher in a whisper.

"Take it in your right hand," instructed the usher. "And repeat after me . . ."

"I swear by Almighty God that the evidence that I shall give to the court shall be the truth, the whole truth and nothing but the truth." The small man blinked up at the judge.

Trelawney sagged gracefully, searching for the bench with his hand. "Look at me, please Mr. Adler. What is your full name?"

"Mark Antony Adler, my lord."

"Are you a bookmaker residing at 100 Fendale Court, Shepherd's Bush?"

"I am, my lord."

Trelawney smiled. "You mustn't call me 'my lord.'

82

My lord might take it for an infringement of his preroga-
tive." There was a three-cornered ploy of private amusement. As if, thought Steel, judge and the two counsel
enjoyed some exquisite joke that was lost on the rest
of them.

"At about ten-thirty on the night of 11th August of
this year, can you remember where you were, Mr. Adler?"

There was no hesitation. "Yes, I can. At the dogs.
White City Stadium."

"Did you have occasion to leave the stadium shortly
after that time?"

Adler's voice was loud. "Yes—my clerk told me . . ."

Trelawney stopped him with a wave. "You're not to
tell us what anyone else said, Mr. Adler. Tell my lord and
the jury, in your own words, what happened after you
left the stadium."

The little dark man had not looked at the dock once.
He kept both hands on the wooden ledge in front of him.
"I come out of the track with my clerk, sir. Where we
was parked was over near the entrances to the council
flats. We 'ad a hundred yards to walk to the car. Being
Vase night . . ."

Judge Croxon leaned down towards Adler. "Do you
say 'being *Vase* night', Mr. Adler?"

"The Vase, m'lord," interjected Trelawney, "I understand to be an important race at the White City Stadium."

Adler continued. "Being Vase night, the City was
packed. People had left their cars all over the place," he
complained. Clarke leaned his head back and yawned
pointedly. It seemed to bring Adler back to his tale.
"Anyway, we was no more than twenty yards from our
car when this other car starts up." He lifted his shoulders
dramatically and let them drop. "After that, everything
happened in a sort of rush, if you know my meaning.
There was a couple of loud bangs—explosions, you might

83

call them. Then somebody started hollering 'Help! He's shot me!'—and another car come tearing by. It almost put us into the wall. And that was it," he finished.

"Yes," Trelawney said softly. "These explosions—could you see where they came from?"

Adler was patient. "From the car I'm telling you about. A man with a pistol."

"It passed very close to you, you say. Were you able to see who was driving it?"

"Yes," Adler said with assurance. "Yes, it was 'im over there." Now he swung his head round at the dock, glasses glinting as he nodded. " 'im," he repeated.

"The one in the civilian clothing?" asked Trelawney.

"The one in the civilian clothing," Adler agreed.

In spite of the inevitability of the denouement, the court was dead silent in the space between Trelawney sitting and Clarke standing.

Steel had been keeping his eyes on Sullivan's back. There had been no change in its position during the whole of Adler's evidence. From Sullivan's pose there was no way of telling if Adler's story was true. Steel let his mind go back to the night of 11th August. He'd been in bed when Sullivan had 'phoned, after eleven. It had taken a quarterhour to dress again and drive to Queen's Gate. Sullivan was waiting in his car, by the Albert Hall 'phone booths. Steel climbed in beside him.

In the dim light, Sullivan's face was calmer than it had been for weeks. Since the night Kosky had crept up to him with the knife. "I've just done Kosky, mate." Sullivan's statement was that of a wrong righted. He tossed a paper bag at Steel. "Here's your gun back, Gerry. Better dump it. I'm going home to wait for the law."

"How badly's he hurt?"

Sullivan shrugged. "I didn't wait to see."

Steel had sat there, watching the rear lights of Sullivan's

car into the westbound traffic. He put on his gloves and opened the bag. The barrel of the automatic was still acrid with burnt powder. He checked the magazine. There were two shells missing.

It had been a hot, fine night. Along the Embankment, the couples still sat close on the benches. Steel drove the length of the river frontage, from Chelsea to the City. Half-a-dozen times, he stopped the car, ready to carry the bag to the river and jettison it. As many times, a sudden movement from the shadows sent him back to the car, guiltily casual. It was after one in the morning when he took the gun back to Draycott Place and buried it. After his arrest, Sullivan had never referred to the happenings of that night. To Sheila, to Galt or to Steel. The accusation that her husband had shot Kosky was hardest for Sheila to live with. Lacking the others' cynical acceptance of the truth, she still sensed it. The realization battered at her security—troubled her loyalty. As if, thought Steel, she were not sure on whose side she *should* be, come hell or high water. No: only Sullivan and this cockeyed little bastard in the witness box knew whether the testimony were true.

Clarke was scanning his notes, making Adler wait. His first question was pleasantly voiced. "Mr. Adler— we haven't had the benefit of your testimony till to-day. But you know, over eight weeks have gone by since 11th August. When did you first tell the police that you had information that might be of use to them?"

The bookmaker's shoulders went back, an improbable attempt to square them. "Four days ago. When Detective-Inspector York come round to my place, asking . . ."

Clarke's voice was a little deeper. "Why not before?"

"Well—same as anyone else, I read all about it, the next day. The papers was full of it. Then I 'eard that it was Kosky and 'im." He jerked his head at Sullivan.

85

"But you knew a crime had been committed," Clarke pointed out, mildly. "Didn't you feel it your duty to go to the police then? You know, you tell us you actually saw the shots fired!"

"Not once I knew them two was mixed up in it." Adler was definite. "Let 'em blow one another's heads off, I thought. But leave me out of it."

Croxon's horsehead peered over the edge of the bench. "But that's hardly a reason for failing to tell the police what you say you saw, Mr. Adler. Don't you know that *failure* to do so is an offence?"

Adler, apparently, had another reason. "I didn't want no razor work done on me, my lord," he said simply.

Clarke puffed contempt at the preposterousness of the answer. "If you felt yourself to be in danger, you could have applied for police protection. Did anyone threaten you?"

The bookmaker shook his head. "They didn't 'ave to. I knew enough about both of them to mind my own business," he finished doggedly.

Clarke's smile at the jury was fat with amusement. "We've heard that before, you know. Then something must have happened since that made you—more public-spirited, I was about to say—less frightened is possibly more correct."

Adler's hands found the printed card on the ledge before him. He moved its length from end to end between nervous fingers. "The police come to see me . . ." he said weakly.

"When you say 'police', whom do you mean, Mr. Adler?"

Adler avoided looking at the table where the detectives were sitting. "Detective-Inspector York, sir."

"And after his visit, you remembered all this!" Clarke waved disdain. He waited till the court was absolutely silent. His voice almost casual, he asked: "How many times have you been in prison, Mr. Adler?"

Trelawney was on his feet before the bookmaker had time to answer. "M'lord," he appealed. "If m'learned friend persists in this line of questioning, I have no alternative but to adopt a certain course."

Every head in the court was turned towards counsel's bench, Steel's included. He knew precisely what this challenge of Trelawney's meant. In a criminal trial, the prosecution was never allowed to bring out an accused man's previous convictions until he was found guilty. Unless—and this was what Clarke had done—the defence deliberately attacked the character of a Crown witness. From that moment, both sides were free to throw whatever dirt they had.

In spite of the hint that Galt had given, the sudden switch of tactics came as a shock to Steel. But possibly, he reasoned, it was a smart move. For two months, the newspapers reporting police court proceedings and the first trial had made certain that the public had no illusions as to the character of either prosecutor or defendant in this case. Maybe Clarke was turning a debit into a credit.

The bookmaker was still scratching the back of his neck. "You got no right . . ." he started. He looked at the judge appealing.

"It isn't for me to suggest what line you should take, Mr. Clarke," said the judge. "But there are certain possibilities that I am sure you have considered." The bony head seemed to wobble with mild disapproval.

"I'm afraid I shall have to persist, my lord." Clarke was adamant.

The judge waved his pen. "Very well. You must answer the question, Mr. Adler."

The dark man's voice was hoarse. "Three times and the last was twenty years ago."

Clarke fronted the jury, confidently. Steel could see that for the first time, Felton was sitting up in his seat, showing interest. "Exactly," agreed Clarke. "Your place of business at the White City Stadium, stand or pitch, whichever it's called, isn't it determined by Mr. Kosky, the prosecutor?"

"The Stewards give me my pitch," asserted Adler.

Clarke nodded. "I'm sorry—I'm not making myself clear, obviously. We know that the stewards allocate a certain number of positions to approved bookmakers and that they, in turn, pay a rental fee. What I'm talking about is the *position* of that pitch. One that is in the front would be more desirable than one at the back—is that correct?"

"You'd get more business, proberly," Adler admitted.

Clarke leaned back, both hands resting on the top of the seat behind him. "And isn't Mr. Kosky the gentleman who says *where* you must put your board and easel— the various things you use in your business of bookmaking—*isn't* he?"

Adler watched Clarke with cagey dislike. "That's right. But he ain't no friend of mine," he said cautiously. "I never spoke to 'im in my life."

Clarke rested his weight comfortably. "We know that Mr. *Sullivan* isn't a friend of yours, at any rate." He glanced at the sketch that Galt had passed to him. "I understand that you have been betting at the White City Stadium for six years, Mr. Adler. Up until two weeks ago your pitch was rather to the rear, away from what you tell the court is the most desirable position. Two weeks ago, you started doing business in the very front row. Is that correct?"

The bookmaker took off his glasses and wiped them before answering. "A couple of people wasn't betting those nights," he mumbled.

88

Clarke was not to be denied. "In fact, the very night that the police came to see you—to suggest that you might be able to help the court in this case—the pitch that you use at the White City Stadium was changed for the better. Am I right?"

Adler's head moved like a tormented animal. "You make it sound . . ."

Clarke's voice now had a biting edge. "Make it sound like what, Mr. Adler? Too much like the truth? Wasn't this it—you were a man with criminal convictions, anxious to curry favour with the police. So you invented this story of seeing this affray—Mr. Sullivan—all these cars careering over the place. And as a reward, Mr. Kosky presented you with a better place of doing business at the White City Stadium?"

Like a snake's, Adler's tongue licked over his lips. "It's a lie," he whispered.

"It's a pack of lies, your story, every single word of it, Mr. Adler," Clarke challenged. "I am bound to put it to you that you did not see Mr. Sullivan at the White City that night. And that you are deliberately perjuring yourself here, for two reasons. Fear and greed. Isn't that the truth, Mr. Adler?"

The bookmaker managed to pack hate into the monosyllable. "No."

Clarke's contempt was magnificent. "No more questions." His little gesture to the jury was amazement at the evil of man. He sat down.

The bookmaker made his way to the back of the court. He sat with the other Crown witnesses who had given evidence, his face twitching with anger. As the bookmaker passed the jury box, it seemed to Steel that Felton's face was sceptical.

It was almost one when the court recessed. Steel walked with Sheila to the pub across the street. They stood at the bar with beer and sandwiches. She had scarcely spoken to him since they had met that morning. He stood, facing the door. After a while, York and two other detectives came in and pushed their way through to the bar. Steel could have stretched out a hand and touched them. They were apparently amused at the evidence of the morning.

"Let's get out of here," Steel said suddenly. He knew that his voice was too loud—too uncertain with anger. His hand in the small of her back, he made her go through to the door. They stood for a moment, outside on the sidewalk. He wiped the sweat from the back of his neck. "I'm sorry, Sheila. I just can't take those bastards. Cops," he said bitterly. "They'll lie, steal, blackmail. Anything people like me are supposed to do. But with them it's all right. They're only trying to get a conviction."

Offices were emptying. Groups of lunch-snatchers rounded the corner, jostling them.

"I want to talk to you," Sheila said suddenly.

He looked down, making his face blank. "Can't it wait?"

She shook her head. "There's plenty of time. It's only twenty-past one."

Never before had he noticed how firm her mouth really was. Until Sullivan's arrest, Sheila had always been what people called a happy girl. Even when she didn't understand, she laughed a lot. Her face, in repose had been quiet, almost grave. Yet never particularly dominant. A man's woman—rather, Sullivan's woman, Steel had always thought. With her, life stopped at her garden gate. It was the way she wanted it. For her, home and family represented the only sane and sure values. As a woman, she was obliged to extend them to her husband's friend. With an enthusiasm that Steel took for smugness, even Sullivan joined in the quest to get Steel

90

married, married to what Sheila described as a "decent girl who'll give you a home."

A home. A cardboard house with little sticky fingers, the silken snare that surely strangled. The thought had been enough to keep Steel clear of the Sullivan home except on ceremonial occasions. He remembered a quiet, soft girl with a readiness for laughter and found the girl beside him almost a stranger.

He nodded across at the churchyard on the other side of the street. "O.K. That's as good a place to talk as anywhere. We'll be sure of nobody listening." He tried a smile but there was no response.

They crossed at the lights, climbed a few steps and sat on the rough bench, surrounded by headstones. He took time, lighting a cigarette. He suspected that she was about to quiz him over his meetings with Alan. He had his answers ready and encouraged her with a grin.

Small lines pulled her brows together. "You think I'm pretty naive, Gerry. Oh, but you *do*," she insisted. "I've lived most of my life in the country." She threw a hand in the direction of the court building without looking at it. "This—the sort of life you led—Danny led—all of it was strange to me." She looked out over the heads of the people who passed below. "But I never really cared. Why *should* I! All of it happened before I knew either of you." She put her hand to the back of her neck uncertainly. "Do you think that Danny is doing the right thing?" she asked quietly.

As if the glowing end of his cigarette held some great importance, he turned it over and looked at it. "How do you mean?" he asked curiously.

She shrugged. "I don't know. If he's really guilty it all seems a desperate struggle to turn wrong into right." He smiled and she saw it. "That makes you laugh but it's true. Solicitors—barristers . . ." she put her hand

91

swiftly on his. "Isn't there *ever* a chance for a man who admits he's done wrong? If they'd let Danny go—give him just enough punishment to teach him a lesson then let him go—I think I could make him leave England. We'd take Tim and go somewhere where nobody knew us. Start all over again." Her voice had the force of certainty. "He'd never do another wrong thing all his life, Gerry."

Her complete absence of realism defeated him. He moved uncomfortably on the bench. "You don't have to sell me, Sheila. My bet is that you're right. But it was Kosky who started all this, not Danny. And a man can stand just so much. If Danny hadn't done what he did, his life would have been hell in this town." It was the first time that either had admitted Sullivan's guilt openly to the other. Steel pulled his feet together, lining the points of his toes with precision. "This isn't a nursery, Sheila," he said at last. "That old man on the bench sees Danny as a menace to society. Not a naughty little boy ready to say that he's sorry. Even when he beats this case, people will remember Danny as a man who made crime pay. The public may admire that—but judges don't."

Almost as though she were speaking to herself she went on. "We could go away with whatever we had. Give the money back."

He sat up and slewed in the seat. He found the sincerity he looked for in her face and pitied her. "For the best part of Danny's life, he's had to fight for whatever he's had. Years in those stinking jails for very little money. You're asking him to give up everything that makes your life comfortable—Tim's. In some cockeyed grandstand gesture." He was exasperated and showed it. "The law wants Danny—not because of Kosky. They don't really care if Kosky's head is on or off his shoulders. But this is the first chance that they've ever had at Danny for the Braden Bullion robbery. If he is found guilty, Croxon will throw the book at him, Sheila." He shook his head. "You can't kiss and make up—not in a court, you can't. You've got to fight them the best way you know how." He looked at his watch and got up. "Danny's going to get out of this—that I promise you."

None of the doubt had gone from the grey eyes. The mouth was still as firm. "I don't believe you, Gerry. You'll never convince me that you can escape the consequences of doing wrong by being smart. Slick, you call it. I love Danny. The awful thing is that I don't know the best way to help him."

He brushed the ash from his coat. "By being a little more realistic," he suggested. He jerked his head at the court buildings. "And not expecting to find Sweet Jesus, fount of love and mercy, sitting in gown and wig on the judge's bench." They walked back to the courts in silence.

As they reached the head of the staircase, they met Galt, coming from one of the 'phone booths. Steel let Sheila go on ahead and hurried after the fat lawyer. He matched Galt's shorter strides till they were at the end of the vaulted hall. The lawyer, pompous and impatient, waited for Steel to speak.

"I just wanted to say, about this additional evidence," observed Steel. "If Adler's the best they can do—he should be no trouble, Clarke crucified him."

Galt allowed himself a smirk. "Clarke and I don't make a bad team, do we? I told you I had a line on Adler." His plump hands came up in caution. "But you can never be sure with a jury. Personally I'd say Croxon's summing-up will determine the strength of Adler's evidence. Remember, we haven't *proved* him to be a liar, yet. What we have done is show the jury good reason why he *might* be lying."

Sheila had already gone into the court. Steel looked at

93

his watch. There were a couple of minutes before the case was on.

"I suppose the wounded hero will give evidence this afternoon."

Carefully, Galt polished the lenses of his library spectacles and put them on. He had the blank wise look of an owl. "I shouldn't think so. Trelawney would hardly want Kosky to follow Adler since it looks as if everyone's dirty washing is going to be aired. We'd better go in," he decided.

As they walked to the court entrance Steel spoke on impulse.

"Have you been able to check on Adler's story—find out where he was at ten-thirty that night?"

The lawyer stood aside to let Steel pass. "When my staff are told to do a job, they do it properly—Adler was exactly where he says he was—watching Sullivan at target practice."

The afternoon wore on with a succession of minor technical witnesses for the Crown. A Scotland Yard cartographer—a cop from the crime lab to swear that the soil taken from the shoes Sullivan wore that night was identical with that found round the plane trees at the back of the White City.

The evidence went for the most part unchallenged. From a layman's viewpoint, it was senseless. The courtroom was overheated. The man in the back row of the jury box still sat, his eyes closed, arms crossed over his chest. Whenever judge or counsel was moved to laboured humour, the jury's smiles were of relief rather than amusement.

Steel concentrated on Felton who lolled in his seat like a party guest at a bad play—bored yet unable to leave. Heat—nerves, kept Steel uneasy on the hard bench. It was like being in a schoolroom with the time till freedom being ticked off ponderously by the clock on the wall behind him. An hour or so and he'd be having a show-down with Felton. Now the time was near, fresh doubts crowded into his head. Felton's wife had been looped last night. Maybe she garbled all that stuff about taxes—Felton doing work abroad and never declaring the money. Perhaps he'd missed some key phrase that turned the conversation into no more than a drunken woman's threat. Then the memory was strong of an open palm on flesh—the flat accusing tone of the woman's voice after-wards. She *had* to be telling the truth. He sneaked a look at Sheila—her eyes were never off the figure in the dock. It would have been easier if there'd been someone else to talk things over with—everyone had ideas of what was best for Sullivan—Sheila was hopeless—the talk in the churchyard made certain he could never tell her about Felton. She was awash with the Never Too Late To Mend slop. A neat helpmate at a time like this, *she* turned out to be. Sullivan would have done better had he married some pig from a slum.

It was twenty-past four and the waiting was unbearable. He leaned over, pulling sticky hands from the varnished wood. "I'm shoving off, Sheila," he whispered. Keeping his head bent, he pushed by to the end of the row.

CHAPTER VII

THE street was grey and wet with a light that was fading fast. He turned the corner taking the driving rain in his face gratefully. A gnome in an oilskin was waiting in the hut by the entrance to the car park. "Much more of this

95

and I'll be growing web-feet," he grumbled. Steel gave the man the ticket, "I'm not going out for a minute. I'm waiting for somebody."

Felton's car was in its place, unoccupied. It was another five minutes before Alan came sloshing across the muddy ground. Steel sounded the horn. Alan climbed into the Zephyr, looking at his shoes with distaste. "You certainly choose the places to meet, Gerry!" He nodded across the car park. "Hey, there's Felton's car!" he said quickly.

Steel sucked in the strong smoke and released it with regret. "I know it. You're full of enthusiasm again," he added sarcastically.

Alan was not at ease. "Sheila's started asking questions. I'm not a lot of good at lying." He sagged—dispirited—"there was more of it to do at the Studio. They wanted to know why I had to leave at four—don't look like that!" Alan's voice rose. "Can't you understand that it's bound to be a bit nerve-wracking at first—that business last night . . ."

Conscious of what was behind his own irritability, Steel was patient. "Sheila doesn't have any idea, does she—what we're doing?"

Alan shook his head. "God, no. I'm not completely helpless, Gerry." He went on uncertainly—"about last night—I didn't know what happened. They were round the corner and on me before I knew it. Was everything all right, Gerry?"

Steel had no intention of going into details. "Nothing happened I couldn't take care of." He chose his words carefully, unwilling to invest them with too much danger. "Look, Alan, in a few minutes, Felton's going to pick his car up. If he's alone we're going to follow him. You'll drive."

"O.K." Alan hesitated. "Just follow. That's all you want me to do?"

Steel smiled assurance. The kid's nerve was still an unknown quantity. "Just follow. Leave the rest to me."

Outside the warm safety of the car, stair rods of rain pelted the earth, washing the metallic cinders free of yellow mud. Straight ahead, the court buildings were sombre with sickly squares of light showing here and there. The copper dome, its figure of justice—blindfolded with her balance—was lost in the rain and cloud. Over in the churchyard a clock struck the half-hour. Already, men were hurrying into the car park, brief-cases clutched under their arms. Steel switched on the motor and hit the wiper control. He peered through the swishing arcs at the street. In a while, Felton came into the car park at a run, holding a sodden newspaper over his head.

Steel moved over to let Alan take the wheel. "Keep as close behind him as you can," he instructed. "But don't make yourself obvious."

The Vauxhall turned out of the park. As Alan gunned the motor, the wheels of the Zephyr spun with sudden power. Gathering traction, the car shot forward. Steel leaned back. His hands were pushed against the dash as if he could slow the speed of the car with the motion.

"*Without* making yourself obvious!" he said.

Felton took the Vauxhall west, past the junction of Hatton Garden and High Holborn, into the narrowing stream of traffic headed for the West End. They were two cars behind, now, with Alan driving on his brakes. Every few yards, he looked up at the driving mirror. As if, thought Steel sourly, the whole of the Yard were on their tail. A bus swung out from a halt, interposing its length between the two cars. Steel touched a light to a fresh cigarette, hiding the shake in his hand. He had no further excuse for postponement. Felton was alone in his car and there was nobody following him—except Steel and his partner.

97

Steel sat straighter, giving instructions without turning his head. "As soon as the lights are against us, pull up beside Felton. Don't pay any attention to me—I'm getting out." He put his key ring on the seat. "Take the car back to Draycott Place and go in and wait."

Thirty yards ahead, the traffic lights at Tottenham Court Road changed from green to amber. Ignoring the warning arm in the cab of a bus, Alan swung the Zephyr wide and cut in front. His front cracked a little and he had to repeat himself. "All right. How long do you want me to wait?"

They were at the lights, abreast of and inside the Vauxhall. Beyond Alan's set face, Steel could just make out Felton at the wheel. The juror's eyes were on the traffic lights.

"Stay there till nine," said Steel. "If I'm not back by then, go home. Whatever happens, don't say anything—do anything—till you hear from me." He pulled on his gloves and put his hand on the door handle. "If you don't hear—I'm pinched. Then you know nothing."

He opened the nearside door and walked round to the back of the Zephyr. For a second he stood in the downpour, waiting. As the lights changed from red to green, he thumbed the catch on the front door of the Vauxhall and got in beside Felton. Horns were blaring in the lane behind. On the left, the Zephyr shot forward then into the Charing Cross Road.

After that first swift look of surprise, Felton showed no emotion at all. He put the car in gear and drove slowly into Oxford Street.

Steel kept his voice quiet. He gripped the door handle ready to jerk it open. "Keep going the way you are. It isn't a hold-up. It's about Anne. Drive into Hyde Park."

The car swerved as Felton turned the wheel towards the kerb. A cab's brake screeched. Steel straightened the wheel with a jerk. "Use your head!" he warned. "I'm not playing games."

Without answering, Felton increased his speed and headed west for the park. At the Bond Street traffic signals, a cop stood on the island, a yard from the window on Felton's side. As if engaged in some joint conspiracy, both men stared straight in front of them. At Marble Arch, the lights blocked them again. Felton spoke for the first time. "Do we want any particular part of the park—or can the drama be played anywhere?" The juror was smiling.

For the first time, Steel noticed the play of the square wrists, the powerful slope of the shoulders. Memory of the lighted hall and Felton motionless in front of a closed door hardened Steel's voice. "Anywhere. Just inside the arch will do. It's well-lighted."

It seemed that Felton smiled without effort. He turned the car into the park and stopped in the carriage way opposite Speaker's Corner. Very leisurely, he reached for the car keys and pocketed them. Then, swinging his body so that he half-faced Steel, the juror waited, still smiling.

Steel took his hand away from the door. He had expected Felton to show fear. Its absence was more than a challenge—it made Steel unsure. Automatically, he offered the blue pack to the other man who took a cigarette without speaking. Under cover of dragging smoke into his lungs, Steel concealed his embarrassment. His uplifted hand was almost a gesture of appeasement.

"I found an old notice of your marriage," he lied. "That's where I got your wife's name. It was a gimmick to get you to listen to me."

Felton settled his weight more comfortably against the door at his back. "I write for a living," he said. "But if I turned in a yarn like this—strangers slipping into one's car at the lights—mysterious Americans with nervous

fingers . . ." He brought the cigarette up slowly, savouring its smell. "A publisher would toss it back at me as
being contrived—improbable. If this isn't a hold-up or
blackmail—" He managed to frown and grin at the same
time. "Americans are ingenious fellows—perhaps you're
selling something?"

Steel felt that he'd lost the initiative. He had a sudden
urge to destroy this man's composure. On the sidewalk,
a few dogs hunched in wet misery, were being exercised
by their owners. A couple of policewomen sauntered by in
the rain, their swinging buttocks mocking their officialdom.
Yet Felton made no move to call for assistance. He merely
bided his time, faintly amused.

"You're on a jury," Steel said suddenly. "I'm interested
in seeing the man in the case go free."

"Ahah!" It was impossible to see Felton's eyes in that
dim light but his voice showed a livened interest. "Isn't
this rather risky for you?" he asked mildly. "Moral
implications apart, aren't you interfering with the course
of justice or something? How do you know that I won't
call the police, for instance?"

They sat probing one another for a moment in the
darkness. Steel sought to inject certainty rather than
menace into his words. "You can forget the moral issues—
they don't come into it. I don't think you have any
intention of calling the police. Because you're not sure
who I am. Or how much I know," he added impulsively.

Felton's irony was pronounced. "How much you know?"
he queried. "I won't bother asking about what—what
you're asking me to do must be a felony. Presumably,
you have a better reason for your friend to go free than
merely *wanting* it?"

Steel hunched his shoulders. *Was* there a better reason
for anything than wanting it! "Maybe," he said slowly.
"I'm ready to pay for the favour, for instance." He

pictured the detached smile the other would be wearing. "If you want still better reasons," he added, "I might be able to come up with one."

As if formality would add point to his words, Felton touched the dash, lighting the interior of the car. He was no longer smiling. "I don't know who you are, my friend. Nor am I particularly interested. But you ought to know more about me since you took the trouble to find out— I don't like being threatened, for instance. Not even mildly threatened. Get out and if I see you again I'll give you in charge."

The hand on Steel's knee had become five steel probes that dug into the nerves behind his kneecap, paralyzing the lower part of his leg. Somehow, he controlled his face to show neither fear nor pain. But the back of his shirt was cold with sweat. He noticed the shake in his hand with vague distaste.

"Out!" ordered Felton.

Steel twisted his face away, unwilling that the other should see his humiliation. His conceit, rubbed raw, urged him to blast this bland face with the truth. To stop him dead with the same words the man's wife had used the night before. But, now, the scene in Felton's house was remote, lacking in conviction. The woman's words preposterous. He leaned hard on the door catch and opened it. Outside, he put his hands on top of the open window, supporting his weight. He spoke impulsively, trying to regain ground.

"You're a man of the world, Felton. This case isn't what they'll make you believe. Sullivan isn't on trial for shooting Kosky. If both of them were dead, the cops would declare a holiday." Feeling was coming back, stabbing his flesh with a million needles. He took his weight on his good leg. "Don't ever think this trial's going to have anything to do with justice, if that's what's worrying you. They're going to jail Sullivan for his share in the Braden Bullion Robbery."

Reaching across, Felton started winding up the window. "Your friend sounds an accomplished rascal. I feel I'll take a lively interest in the case now. Good night." He let in the clutch suddenly.

As the Vauxhall moved away, Steel fell to his knees, bone grinding into the wet sidewalk. He stayed there for a second, watching the tail light of Felton's car. Aware of the two patrolling policewomen, he managed to get to his feet, brushing the mud from his trousers. Then he limped across the carriage-way, away from official female scrutiny and into the peace of the dark, pointing trees. The wet soil and grass sucked at his feet, smearing his socks. He kept walking, in spite of the pain. Less to think than to avoid thought in physical movement.

He passed the bandstand where aged whores moved furtively from one vantage point to another. He found a cab in the South Carriage Way and paid off at the corner of Markham Square. It was still raining. Screened by the bushes and trees, he made the circuit of the square. Felton's car was parked in front of his house. A light shone in the drawing-room.

He walked back to Draycott Place. It was unlikely that Felton had gone to the police. There had been no time. What he did in the future was anyone's guess. Steel waited on the corner of Sloane Avenue, lighting a cigarette in the shadow of somebody's doorway. His own car was parked in from of his rooms. There was no sign of a police car. He used the street door with care. Upstairs, his own front door was open and the place in darkness. He called softly. "Alan?"

There was movement from a chair by the window. Alan got to his feet, his drawn face plain in the light from the street lamp. "Are you all right, Gerry?" He spoke in a whisper as if calamity trailed Steel.

Steel found the light button. He threw curtains across the windows. His answer was snarled. Here, he was surer of himself. "Of course I'm all right. Go on home." He made no attempt to explain.

Alan crossed to the fireplace while Steel took the armchair. Shamefaced, the younger man searched for words that would excuse. "I can't go on with this, Gerry. It's no use." He lit a cigarette, gulping the smoke as he paced from the door to the fireplace. Suddenly he stopped. "Well say it and get it over!" he shouted. "Don't just sit there! All right, I'm a coward—I'm anything you want to call me. But I just can't *do* it, Gerry!" He threw the cigarette at the fire and came over to Steel. "I'm sorry, Gerry. I'll go. Here are your keys." He held out the keyring.

Steel looked up from the chair, heavy-eyed and aware of the uselessness of criticism. They had something, this boy and his sister, that put them irrevocably on the other side of the fence. He got to his feet and put his arm round the other's shoulder. "Forget it, Alan," he said quietly. "I should never have asked you in the first place." He dug his fingers into the other's flesh. "One thing. I expect you never to say a word to anybody about what has happened."

Alan put out his hand. "I won't, Gerry . . ." he shrugged. "Good luck," he said uncertainly.

Steel nodded. When the door had closed, he sat in the chair for a while. Ah well, that was that. From there on, he was on his own. He undressed in the tall, narrow room and lay on the bed in the dark. Like a dog, he thought. Like a beaten dog in a corner. The night was sour with the memory of Felton's mocking smile. The juryman's fingers, crippling tendons. Worst of all was the new uncertainty. Now, he had committed himself.

At this second, Felton might be in his sitting-room, smiling over the scene in the park. Extracting its full dramatic value. And in another moment, he might cross the red carpet to the telephone.

Steel tensed as a car slowed outside, its lights sweeping the ceiling and walls. But it passed. He crawled under the bedclothes and closed his eyes. It was too late to do anything but go on. Now, it was a power-play between Felton and him. There could be no compromise. Just victory or defeat. After a while he slept.

The night had taken the rain, leaving a washed white morning sky. He stood by the window, the electric razor buzzing in his hand. The old bat downstairs had awakened him at eight, her voice over the 'phone, crackling with venom.

". . . and you've got to be out, Mr. Steel, with all your belongings. I'll accept no more rent after Saturday." Defeated by his silence, she'd paused. Then her voice became shriller. "The owners have told me how to deal with you, Mr. Steel. Mr. Steel! Do you hear? I'm going to call the *police* if you give me any more trouble."

Very carefully, he had worked the receiver rest up and down with a finger, hoping it might break her ear drum. Then he replaced the head set.

He felt his chin gingerly. There was still the importance of appearance. The curtains blowing in front of him were grimed with winter dirt. Down below, faceless people scurried out of the rooms that passed for homes, headed for bus or subway. Christ! he thought. It's been so long now. The hot, fierce brightness of a tropical day, the smell of rotting fruit and the ammoniac reek of the whitewashed walls. Well, if he ever came out of this with his liberty, he'd give the job another year then pull out. There was nothing to hold him in England. Somewhere a man must be able to make a living in warmth and with an easy mind.

104

He took the usual route to the Old Bailey and parked in the bomb site. Felton's Vauxhall was already there, by the side of the attendant's shack. Steel went down, past the carrion crew at the Public Gallery entrance, up the steps at the front to the courts. Sheila was waiting and came across the hall as she saw him.

Always graceful, he thought. The mixture of cat and mother that he should have married himself. Part of his brain winced at the word marriage. *Sure*, it whispered. *Marry someone like Sheila. Make some good woman happy!*

He took Sheila's hand and tucked it into the warm crook of his arm. Since that talk in the churchyard Sheila was quieter, more relaxed. No longer did she hit him with questions that had no answers but sat on the bench, watching the dock. Almost complacently now, as if, secretly, she were as sure of her husband's acquittal as Steel himself. Womanly intuition, may be, Steel thought. It was one of the few things that it paid to respect in a woman's make-up. And yet there was nothing he could do to add to her assurance. Since last night he was completely alone. Not even to Sullivan could he pass the word. And Galt would run a mile if he thought that he was even remotely connected with an attempt to fix a juror. It was too raw, too improbable—the lawyer's chief objection would be that Steel's scheme could never succeed. Steel imagined Galt's voice, honey-lemon as it was when used for sarcasm. "Fix a juryman! Do you think this is Chicago, Gerry? Why not try Judge Croxon while you're about it—for God's sake let's be thorough!" And the fat arm would be a weight on Steel's shoulders—then the voice again, syrup-smooth now. "There's only one way to beat them, my boy—in court!"

By now, Steel recognized people who were taking the same seats in the court every day. The woman over in the privileged stalls. Sleek with mink and provocative under her mauve feather cap. She brought a touch of detached elegance to the desperate struggle for a man's liberty. Then the man like a Rugby player, two benches away. Salt and pepper tweeds and a yellow tie. His red face was turned eagerly towards the top of the stairs that Sullivan would climb in a moment. A sophisticated woman—a farmer, both of them held by the drama of trial by judge and jury.

Like a school prefect, stuffy with delegated authority, the Clerk of the Court read the jury roster. All were present. Felton was in blue and answered his name with the usual air of being mildly amused by the proceedings.

Behind the judge's bench a door opened. The usher's voice bawled. The court was filled with a sound of scraping feet. Steel stood with the rest of them, bending slightly so that a shoulder hid his face from Felton. Though it was morning, the electric lights burned. If you ignored the ticking clock on the wall behind, the room was timeless. Croxon took his seat, inclining his long bony head as the clerk stood to whisper. There was silence elsewhere but the two voices shushed on meaninglessly. Then the old man's words were clear. He addressed the foreman of the jury.

"I understand that you have a communication from one of the jury that you wish to hand to me."

The foreman got to his feet a little sheepishly. "Yes, my Lord. One of my colleagues has asked me to pass this up."

The usher took the proffered envelope and carried it to the judge. There was complete silence now in the court. From counsels' bench, Clarke and Trelawney watched the judge intently. The two detectives turned their heads round, peering frankly at the jury.

Involuntarily, Steel was half out of his seat. He had no doubt what this envelope contained—or which member

106

of the jury had sent it up. It was the dramatic sort of gesture that would appeal to Felton. Denouncement in open court. The juryman must have seen him come in, waited till Steel sat down, then scribbled the note.

Steel forced himself back in his seat. It was too late now to try to get out of the court. Police, ushers, covered all the exits. Outside would be a nightmare of echoing passages. Running footsteps and over your head, the metallic voice of the Public Address system. "STOP THAT MAN!"

Vaguely, he knew that Sheila was whispering something but he had no reply for her. He put a dry tongue across dryer lips and closed his eyes as if, by shutting out the scene in front of him, he might change it.

Still unflurried, the voice from the bench continued. Croxon's mild tone opened Steel's eyes. The judge half-turned in his seat and Trelawney and Clarke listened attentively as the judge addressed them.

"I have a request from one of the jury that they might be allowed to visit the car park at the White City Stadium. In a case of this kind, it may be that first-hand knowledge of the scene would assist the jury to arrive at a proper verdict." Thin, white hands joined and the voice brooked no hope of argument from counsels 'bench. "This afternoon would seem a suitable time for this to be done, Mr. Trelawney."

The prosecutor stood. "If it please, m'lord. I intend calling Mr. Kosky as my next witness. Examination-in-chief should not take too long. We might be able to finish with this witness this morning." The actor's smile was for Clarke. "Subject to my learned friend's cross-examination."

Clarke was not ready for humour. "From the defence point of view, m'lord, this afternoon is entirely suitable. Mr. Galt has already been over the terrain. I shall take

107

the opportunity of doing so myself." He sat down.

There was the sense of living again. The old, slightly sickening relief that came when you had passed a stationary prowl car and no voice called from within. The wet-handed haste as you dropped into cover of night while, behind you, bells rang and lights came on in a house now alarmed. Still unable to bring himself to watch Felton, Steel concentrated on the other side of the court.

At the head of the stairs leading down from the dock, one of the two warders had been waiting his cue. Now he beckoned. There were footsteps and Sullivan's head showed against the glass surround. As he saw Sheila, the uncertainty left his face. He smiled and Sheila smiled back. In the space of that brief recognition, it seemed to Steel, Sullivan and his wife were beyond the reach of everyone in the court. Including me, thought Steel. Theirs was an understanding beyond the Code. It was a reflection that Steel found disturbing. Sullivan took his seat between the two warders. From the angle of his head, Steel knew that his friend was watching Croxon.

It had been days now since Steel had been up to Brixton Prison. There had been neither time nor reason for more visits. In any case, the fifteen minutes a day belonged to Sheila and Sullivan. In spite of Sullivan's love for his wife, Steel knew the way the man reacted. The look he had given Sheila was not just affection. With years of your life at stake, the uppermost emotion was fear. Yet, Sullivan showed none. Somehow, Sheila must have managed to reflect Sullivan's own confidence in his lawyers, reinforce her husband's hope. Whatever else she'd done, she'd used the visiting periods sensibly these past few days.

He found her arm with new warmth glad to forget her pessimism of the previous day—seeing the grave, handsome face with fresh enthusiasm. Sheila was all right. The wish to tell her so—the unvoiced assurance that he was going to get Sullivan free—these went into the rough pat that he gave her arm.

Beyond her, the red-faced man in tweeds stared at Sullivan as if he expected to see two heads on one pair of shoulders. In the privileged stalls, the fashionably-dressed woman masked her interest with concern for her make-up.

"Call Edward Kosky," said Trelawney.

By the witnesses' waiting-room, the usher gave the summons new importance. "Edward Kosky," he shouted, pulling open the door. A few heads craned from the public gallery. In the press box a couple of reporters exchanged superior smiles of inside knowledge.

Steel knew these reporters—feature men on a couple of dailies. Equally at home in the press room at Scotland Yard and the pubs along Whitehall—in the bars where they bought Flying Squad Officers drinks in return for stale, uninspired information. Less convincingly at home in the pubs and clubs fashionable among successful thieves. There, they were glib with first names, bright with the use of thieves' patter always just a little out-of-date. It was a strange breed of man who sacrificed everyone's interests save their own to the need for a story.

Kosky's entrance to the court was a tribute either to the Crown Solicitor's instructions or to his own sense of the fitting. He squared his bulky shoulders without swagger and made his way to the witness box where he covered his head reverently as he took the oath. A clean bandage was wound about his forehead. He answered Trelawney's first question with quiet respect.

Few in the court had not read of the career of this son of an East End tailor. He had gone, like a bull-dozer, through the cellar spielers in the Aldgate area, dominating the thieves, gamblers and pimps till, in the East End, only one name mattered. See Kosky, they said.

In him, pride of race was strong. Protecting Jewish gambling interests, Kosky and his mob pushed slowly westwards, challenging the Italians in Soho, the loosely-knit gangs of the South and West. Kosky's rise had paralleled Sullivan's. Sullivan, who by now was the idol of every boy-burglar from the Elephant to the Bush.

Finally, Kosky and Sullivan had combined for strength, each secretly convinced of his own superiority. It was an uneasy alliance that lasted for five years.

You were a bookmaker and wanted a pitch at the dogs—the chance to earn a few quid at a point-to-point—then you saw Kosky, or Sullivan. You owned a drinking club where some whisky-fired bum gave you trouble. A word with the right amount of cash to Kosky, or Sullivan, and the troublemaker was attended to by one of the boys in some dark convenient spot and introduced to a six-inch blade held in the palm of the hand.

In that world where violence carried respect, Kosky and Sullivan were paramount. But you didn't live on respect, pay-offs from small-time bookmakers, still less on the large scotches that greeted your entrance into any of the fifty bars. So, since each man had the characteristics of the successful thief, the partnership extended to the half-dozen coups that ended in the Braden Bullion Robbery. This time, Sullivan's superiority had gone unquestioned. His was the patient acquisition of information, the chronometrical timing, the savage determination to let nothing stand in the light of success.

When he had made his score, Sullivan bowed out. For any thief, given a reason of sufficient strength, can cross the tracks and wipe the eyes of the Christian bawlers of uncharitable slogans. Sullivan's wish to conform was simple. He had the best of one world—his share in the Braden Bullion Robbery. Now he wanted the best of the other—the right to enjoy his loot in peace. There

110

was a simple bar to Sullivan's pursuit of legality. With him, Kosky had made more money than ever before. With Sullivan out of the combination, Kosky was no more than a hammer-throwing thug controlling bums he recruited from Skid Row and the jail house gates. Sullivan retired from the rackets with the dope on half-a-dozen potential crocks of gold—coups that he nursed. Almost overnight, Sullivan was a car dealer. He still had a helping hand for a grafter but his information stayed where it was. In the long square head with its brooding eyes.

It took Kosky a couple of months to decide that Sullivan's information belonged to the partnership—if Sullivan had no more use for it, Kosky had—Sullivan laughed in Kosky's face. A gesture that was repaid with a nine-inch scar on Sullivan's neck. From that moment, Steel knew that Sullivan's conceit would never let him rest.

From the dock to the witness box, the two men looked at one another. Their faces were without expression, only the eyes betrayed their mutual hate.

Somehow, Kosky's posture in the witness box managed to suggest an admission of five previous convictions for crimes involving violence, combined with the readiness to do his civic duty.

Trelawney wasted no time. "Yes, Mr. Kosky. You are a bookmaker residing at 705 Oxford Court, Marylebone?"

"That's right, sir."

"Is part of your occupation the supervision of book-makers' pitches at the White City Stadium?"

"That's right, sir."

As Trelawney bent over the papers in front of him, his fingers touched the wig and the iron-grey curls moved incongruously. "At about ten-thirty-five on the night of 11th August this year, can you remember where you were, Mr. Kosky?"

111

Kosky gave the question fair consideration. "Not so I'd be sure to the minute, sir. But somewhere about then—yes. I was getting out of my car. It was parked behind the track."

"Exactly." Trelawney's quiet, conversational tone created a picture of a warm summer night—you saw cars parked under trees and men going lawfully about their business. "Where did you intend going when you say you were getting out of your car?"

Kosky was still punctilious. "Well, I'd been on the track and I was going home, sir. Then I saw somebody." He hesitated. "So I got out the car again."

Trelawney's thin lips smiled encouragement. "What was it that made you change your mind?"

"I saw Sullivan, sir," Kosky said simply.

"That's the defendant—the man in the dock?" Trelawney was making sure there could be no mistake.

"Yes, sir."

The lawyer shook his hands free from the loose sleeves of his gown, giving the jury the benefit of his determination to hide nothing. "Mr. Kosky—we've heard evidence —no doubt m'friend will deal further with the matter— that you knew the defendant. Do you say that this is correct?"

"Yes, sir. I've known him on and off for—" Kosky looked up at the ceiling, frowning, "ten—or eleven years." His head turned to the dock with a hard blank stare.

"Would you say that you've been friends over this period?" asked the prosecutor.

Kosky shrugged his shoulders with the movement of a fighter between rounds. "I was a friend of his, sir," he said at last. "But I ain't so sure about him being a friend of mine. Not after the night you're talking about, I'm not." This time, he overdid it. The casual touch of the bandage—the padded eyes that crinkled in a smile—

112

both suggested a little too much theatre.

Trelawney's head sagged a little. His eyes were on the witness box and he spoke with regret. "In the past, you have had several convictions for crimes that involved the use of violence. When was the last?" the lawyer finished gently.

Kosky hunched his shoulders again. "Seven years ago. It's not always easy in my line of business, sir. A lot of the time there's trouble on the track and the stewards look to me to keep order." He was suddenly conscious of Trelawney's frown. "When I say keep order, sir, I mean that a word from me can prevent trouble—help the police. These convictions of mine have always been something like that. A fight and me protecting myself."

"Tell my lord and the jury, Mr. Kosky—has the defendant ever been concerned with you either as a confederate or a victim—in *any* way—in any of these convictions?"

"No, sir," Kosky said definitely.

"Have you ever used violence on Sullivan—ever caused violence to be used on him?"

"No, sir."

"Threatened him?"

Kosky shook his head. "I never had cause to threaten him. I always thought he was my friend."

Trelawney used the second's pause to look meaningly at the jury. Then he continued: "Getting back to the night of 11th August. When you got out of your car—you told us it was because you saw Sullivan—had you any reason to feel apprehensive? Afraid?"

Kosky's eyes were wary. He glanced at the judge then at Trelawney and settled his weight back on his heels. "I didn't have *reason* to be afraid, sir. I just saw him sitting there at the wheel of his car and got out to have a chat with him." He paused.

113

"Go on," encouraged Trelawney.

"Well—I started over to his car. I'd gone a few yards when I heard this explosion. At first I thought it was a car back-firing. I remember looking round to see where it had come from. Then I saw the pistol in the . . ." he seemed to be having difficulty finding the right word, "defendant's hand. He was sat with it resting on top of the window which was down." He brought his right hand up and rested it on top of the ledge, cocking his thumb like a trigger. "Like that! There was another explosion and I saw smoke coming out of the barrel. I felt something hit me here"—he touched the bandage again—"then everything happened so quick. Next thing I remember was the doctor at the hospital talking to me."

Croxon's voice interrupted. He leaned down towards the witness box, his thin nose seemingly peaked with distaste. "How well-lighted was this part of the road where you say the defendant's car was parked, Mr. Kosky?"

"It was under a street lamp, sir—my lord. I could see him as plain as if it had been daylight."

"I'm much obliged, my lord," Trelawney said. He turned to the jury. "The street lights are marked on the plan that you'll find in the folders, members of the jury." He turned back to Kosky. "I'd like you to look at this plan, Mr. Kosky. You'll see that the street lamps are marked with a small circle. Under which of these circles do you say that the defendant's car was parked?"

A thick finger hovered then stabbed the heavy drawing paper. "Right here, sir. Where the pavement narrows a bit."

"I see." Trelawney's next question was blunt. "Do you know a Mr. Adler, Mr. Kosky?"

"I do."

"When did you last have occasion to talk to him?"

"It must be a year ago, at least, sir. We know one another but we're not what you'd call friends, sir. I see him at the races and the dogs. I suppose we're what you'd call acquaintances."

"Just acquaintances," agreed the prosecutor. "Have you any idea why Mr. Adler's betting position at the White City Stadium has been changed recently?"

Kosky was completely at ease. "I think I can answer that all right, sir. It was done by someone who works for me—that's how I heard about it. You see, there's some nights when bookmakers in the Silver Ring don't show up. Maybe they're ill or get a losing turn or don't have the money to go on betting. It's rare the same people are betting—all together, I mean. So, when there's one of the good pitches empty, we move up any of the regulars who happen to be there that night."

"So far as you know, Mr. Kosky, Mr. Adler's position was changed in the normal way, by one of your men?"

"That's right, sir."

"One last question, Mr. Kosky. You know the defendant. Is there any doubt in your mind that it was he and nobody else who fired that pistol at you on the night of eleventh August?"

Deliberately, Kosky brought his head round so that he faced the dock. Then he shook his head, with certainty. "There's no doubt whatsoever, sir."

"Thank you, Mr. Kosky." Trelawney sat down.

Beyond the angle of the dock, Steel could just see Felton. As Kosky joined his hands behind his back, pulling down his body and head into a position of caution, the juryman's face was doubtful.

Steel waited for Clarke to crucify this coppering rat! In the momentary hush, the defence lawyer scanned his notes, Steel remembered how Kosky must feel—the frantic scrambling of thought as you tried to outguess a skilled

115

and determined cross-examiner. His face a hostile mask, Steel waited for Clarke to speak.

Defence counsel rose. For a second, he stood with his arms hanging at an angle, like a cormorant drying its wings. His voice was quiet.

"Do you describe yourself as a truthful man, Kosky?"

The dark, heavy jowl tilted. "I think so, sir. I know I'm under oath to speak the truth in this box, if that's what you mean."

"Very well," said Clarke. "Mr. Trelawney asked you about your previous convictions. How many times have you been before a court, Kosky?"

The witness's eyes lowered. "Five times, sir."

Clarke nodded. "For a crime of violence on each occasion? Anything else?"

"No, sir."

At the solicitor's table, Galt's short arm waved a slip of paper that Clarke took. He consulted it. "Let me get this absolutely straight. Nobody's trying to trick you, Kosky. Do you say that you have never been convicted for any other offence except . . ."—he shrugged— "*defending yourself*, I think you called it?"

In his uncertainty Kosky turned towards Trelawney who averted his eyes. "Not for any criminal offence, no. Gambling. A couple of traffic offences. Drunk, once. In my line of business, it's not too easy to keep out of trouble."

"Occupational hazards," Clarke's voice was dry. In the jury box Felton smiled. "Let me refresh your memory, Kosky. I appreciate that it might be difficult for you to keep track of the minor misfortunes attached to your career." He read from the slip of paper. "Marlborough Street Police Court. 28th November, 1946. Edward Kosky. Fined fifty pounds for making a false statement in order to obtain Board of Trade supplementary clothing coupons. Does this conviction refer to you, or not?"

"It wasn't a criminal conviction, sir. That's what I meant when I said no. There was lots of people . . ."

"Then you *were* convicted on this occasion?."

"Yes."

"And you pleaded guilty to this offence?"

"Yes."

"How does making a false statement to get clothing coupons square with your description of yourself as a truthful man?"

Kosky retrieved his hands from behind his back and placed them on the edge of the witness box. For a second, he studied them. "I did no worse than lots of others did, sir. It was just after the war. There was regulations then. People didn't look on that sort of thing as being criminal."

Clarke's face showed polite astonishment. "Indeed? What I'm really getting at is when—as a normally truthful person—do you depart from the truth, Kosky?"

"I *always* try to tell the truth, sir." Pads of flesh on the prominent cheekbones, relics of countless blows, hid Kosky's eyes. He spread a hand in resignation. "Everybody lies, sometime or other."

Clarke was dangerously patient. "You know," he observed mildly, "you seem to be telling my lord and the jury a great deal about what other people do. What we're interested in is what *you* do. I'll put the question in a different form. When do you usually lie?"

Kosky made no reply. When the question came again, with added emphasis, he mumbled. "It's a trick question —how do you expect me to answer—when I'm thinking of myself, I suppose."

"Precisely. Out of motives of self-preservation, in other words. No matter what injustices were done to anyone else, you'd be ready to lie when you think of yourself. Isn't that right?"

117

Blood made Kosky's swarthy face darker but his voice was still stubborn. "I'm not lying now."

Clarke's look at the jury was an appeal to reason. He went back to the witness. "I put it to you that you *are*, Kosky. That your whole story as told here in court is nothing but a parade of deliberate lies. I am bound to criticize the behaviour of the police officers in this case. But it may be that you succeeded in hoodwinking them as you are trying to hoodwink us here, now. You are lying, Kosky, for the reason you, yourself, have given. Self-preservation. Isn't that correct?"

"I'm not lying, sir." Kosky shook his head.

Clarke slammed hard at the point. "Lying because you know perfectly well that somebody else fired that pistol at you that night—somebody you feared then and still fear now. You knew if you involved the real culprit with the police, it would go ill for you among the people you associate with. It was convenient to accuse a man like the man in the dock." Clarke stretched a hand at Sullivan whose eyes had never left Kosky. "Someone you knew to be in bad odour with the police."

The voice was pitched lower but still adamant. "No, sir."

"Very well," said Clarke. "Let's go on to something entirely different."

Clarke's finesse was gone, his cross-examination turned into a frontal attack on Kosky's character. Past and present. Sweat showed under the man's bandage, but his answers remained dogged.

With the exception of Felton, the jurors craned to catch each word, watching as Kosky stalled and spluttered. His neck supported by the back rest, Felton was staring up at the ceiling as if any doubt he held would be resolved there.

Surely, thought Steel, even with a jury like this a man

had a chance. Kosky's was the only real evidence against Sullivan and how *could* his word stand. Tradition among thieves held that the jury which kept its eyes on the man in the dock was a bad one. Already convinced of his guilt, they felt no need to weigh the reactions of any of the witnesses.

Clarke was done at last. He sat down, shaking his head slowly yet avoiding the interested eyes of the jury. It was a dumb yet perfect renunciation of every answer Kosky had made.

Trelawney was brief. "Mr. Kosky. Everyone in this court has heard your remarkably frank admissions to m'learned friend's questions. I don't propose to keep you any longer than it takes to tell me this—you are aware of the nature of the oath you have sworn?"

Kosky's head lowered very slightly. "Yes, sir."

"And has the evidence you have given here this day been the truth, the whole truth and nothing but the truth?" Trelawney's florid manner stressed the triteness of the phrase.

"It has, sir."

"Thank you, Mr. Kosky." Prosecuting counsel looked up at the bench. "May it please my lord, that finishes the evidence for the prosecution."

The judge bent an ear to catch his clerk's whisper. With the deliberation of a judge who invests even the trivial with importance, he scratched in his book. Then he looked up. "Mr. Trelawney, Mr. Clarke. In view of the jury's wish to visit the scene," it seemed as if the voice were edged with annoyance, "I propose to adjourn until half-past ten tomorrow morning." He turned the crescent-shaped spectacles towards the jury box, looking over them. "Members of the jury, arrangements have been made for you to visit the car park at the White City Stadium. It will be practical for you to do this after lunch.

Necessarily, this will delay the trial—adding to the burden that is upon prosecution and defence alike. I am sure you will be mindful of this when making any further request to the court." Twice, he bowed then, still stooped from the shoulders, walked to the door to his chambers.

In the shuffle of movement that followed, Steel found Sheila's arm with his fingers. "I've got some things to do—I'll see you here, tomorrow morning."

She was leaning forward, mouth slightly open, staring at the now empty dock. It was as if she neither heard nor felt him. He tightened his fingers reassuringly and made his way from the building.

CHAPTER VIII

FIRST he had to have Anne Felton's address. It was back at Draycott Place. He cut down to the Embankment. He was driving badly, resentment and frustration spinning the steering wheel just that fraction too much. He missed a cyclist by inches, sending the scared man teetering like a dying top. Losing balance, the cylist scraped frantically at the road with one foot. Steel watched him, safe, to the kerb then took his eye from the driving mirror.

Cut this out, he thought. Next thing, he'd be held on a dangerous driving charge. Shocked at the thought, he drove soberly for the rest of the way. At Draycott Place, the three tall rooms upstairs were oddly unfamiliar. He stood for a moment at the dirt-streaked windows. Beyond, the brown-stone balcony was a welter of hopelessness. The urn where he'd hidden the gun, its chrysanthemums now dying. A few cigarette packages nudged a pile of sodden leaves. To-day, the place was even more depressing than ever. Then he remembered. It was weeks since he had seen the place in the day. Usually, by the time he returned home, dusk and artificial lighting were kind to stained carpets and sagging springs.

Anne Felton's address he had pinned with a thumb tack on the underside of a table. Once this case was over, the hell with living in a place of this kind—the sordidness of genteel London. If an honest living didn't bring you comfort what the hell was its use! There was one thing, this case had proved to him clearly. For a cop, at least, a thief was always a thief. A potential victim for a shake-down. That was the sort of thing you took in the name of security. Security—a cardboard house filled with kids with running noses. A woman whose voice got shriller by the year. Sheila talked of taking Sullivan out of it when the case was over—that'd be the end of Steel's job any-way. Ah well, maybe he could go back to flying—places like Bolivia, El Salvador—they worried less about your past than your take-off.

He ran down the stairs, ignoring a half-dozen memories. In Canada, France had been the answer to a troubled spirit. Yet France proved no more than a spring-board for Italy. A winter in Rome gave him a circle of the phoniest acquaintances a phoney city could produce and the conviction that London would hold what he wanted. Now, as then, he thought he knew what he wanted.

As he passed Mrs. Kolmer's door, it opened. Dewlaps thick with mauve powder quivered as she saw Steel. She watched with venom as he riffed through the pile of mail on the chest in the hall. There was none for him and he looked up smiling. "Not a single postcard," he said. "That's going to kill your afternoon. Never mind—no doubt you'll get the kettle to work later."

Holding the door ready to swing shut, she nodded with

rage. "I'm an *honest* woman and don't you forget it, *Mister* Steel." Her lips went into fifty tiny folds, baring teeth like toothbrush handles. "Everybody in this house is going to be glad to see the back of you."

He paused, pulling on his gloves, tired suddenly of her and all that she stood for. "Look," he said sourly. "If ever I hear the words 'police', 'thief', any one of the expressions you sling at me—if you give me the least bit of a hard time between now and Saturday, you old battle-axe, I'll slap you with something that will really hurt—a slander suit. Now don't *you* forget it, Mrs. Kolmer."

Satisfied with the fear in her eyes, he turned his back and went out to the car.

The Argyle Arms was a red brick apartment building where quiet roads bisect the Outer Circle at St. John's Wood. It was a neighbourhood fashionable with dress manufacturers, Viennese restaurateurs and as popular as Sloane Avenue as a home for wealthy and misunderstood women.

There were six storeys of it, a hundred yards long. A crescent-shaped driveway passed the main entrance. Two uniformed porters stood outside under the portico.

He drove past the block and stopped fifty yards up, where the usual huddle of shops was pretentious with chrome and concave fronts. Anne Felton lived in a block that was hazardous for visitors with larceny in their hearts. Take any front door for a quarter mile—the chances were that behind it would be at least a mink coat. It was the spiritual home of the drummer—the unimaginative thief ready to knock on a hundred doors and tear the first unanswered off its hinges. Insurance companies knew it. Scotland Yard knew it. The porters at the Argyle Arms knew it.

There was a 'phone booth on the corner. He used it, narrowing his nose against the thick stale smell of the place. The number of Anne Felton's apartment was 416. In most modern blocks this was an indication of the floor. Running gloved finger down slowly he scanned all the 'phone numbers having the same exchange. Twice he found names with addresses in the Argyle Arms—379 and 114. These would be third and first floors—he needed fifth or sixth. It took five more minutes to find what he wanted. Karl Hershell, Dental Surgeon, 540 Argyle Arms. Beside the address was the notation *Residence*. Another said *Surgery* with a Wimpole Street number.

It was perfect. If challenged, he'd give the Hershell name, ride up to the fifth floor then walk down to the fourth. For the record, an enquiry at 540 wouldn't hurt. The whole thing was made to order. He'd be a man with a head full of aching teeth, confusing the dentists' home address with that of his surgery.

He left the car on the road where it was hidden from the porters and walked up the gravelled driveway. In the soft lit entrance hall, a couple of beady-eyed reception-ists looked up as the doors swung open. Training prompted Steel to ignore them. His feet without sound on the deep carpet, he crossed to the elevators.

Those zealous in the protection of their masters' property have the less obvious ways of conveying doubt to their fellows. The elevator attendant looked past Steel to the Reception Desk then slid back the doors of the cage.

"What name, sir?" he asked respectfully.

"Mine?" Steel grinned at him. Always he had this mania for forcing people to expose their hands. He regretted it too late.

"What name did you want, sir?" the man said patiently.

"Dr. Hershell, Fifth floor," Steel volunteered.

The door slid shut with trellised ease. Steel held his hat, peering into its crown. Like some bored attendant upon a funeral, he thought. The mechanism whirred then stopped. Without getting out, the man gestured towards his left. "540's at the end, sir, on the outside of the block."

The gates shut. The sound of the dropping cage was an offence to the hushed corridor. The door of 540 differed slightly from its neighbours. A tiny Hebrew scroll was screwed to the jamb at breast height. And why not, he told himself. As propitiation it was decidedly better than "God Bless this House" done in sampler work and hung over the sitting-room fireplace.

He pressed a thumb. Three chimes sounded in the apartment. There was a minute's wait before the door opened. She was dark, this woman, with straight hair pulled back and looped like a twisted loaf at the nape of her neck. 45 years, perhaps, had left her elegance and charm that lit her smile. Her "Good afternoon" had a faint Austrian accent.

"Doctor Hershell?" he asked.

"But he is not here!" The protest was smiling. "This is a personal matter?"

"I'm afraid not." The pleasure of adding convincing detail was strong. "No more personal than a diseased molar."

"Then you must go to Wimpole Street. What a shame! Was it an appointment?"

He shook his head. "In desperate need of one. I'm terribly sorry to have troubled you. I'll 'phone the doctor at Wimpole Street."

The door closed, shutting him out from the fragrant warmth of the interior. For a second he stood, reluctantly envious, then made his way to the elevator shafts. Beside them, a glass door led to a service stairway. He walked down a flight to the fourth floor then along to 416. This time the heavy front door had nothing to distinguish it from ninety-one others on the floor. The locks were bright with chrome and brass but useless as protection. One was a spring, the other a roller lock. He pressed his glove finger against the top of the door and felt it move an inch in play. With a strip of celluloid, he could open it as easily as Anne Felton could with a key.

For the moment, though, getting inside her home was of less importance than gaining an insight into her habits, her haunts. He had to meet this woman casually yet with conviction, in some place public to them both. A woman at the door of her home was much less receptive than she'd be on a bar stool, for instance. Only, if there were no other way of checking her movements, would he break into her flat.

He bent his head, lifting the flap of the mail box and listening. The spring-loaded flap pushed back just far enough to show a strip of hall carpet the other side. There was no sound of movement. Just the quiet of an un-occupied home. Somewhere at the far end of the corridor, round the bend, a door slammed. He walked quietly back to the stairway and ran up to the fifth floor. When the elevator arrived, the attendant grinned recognition. At the fourth again, they stopped to collect the woman who had disturbed Steel.

In the entrance hall, Steel made himself as indifferent to the receptionists' acceptance as he had been to their suspicion and walked out to the street. In the car, he lit a cigarette, pulled a leg up under him and eyed the red brick building sourly. Before he got carried away with himself, just what had the accomplished! Fronted a few porters and managed to get upstairs without a tumble. Then what? You knew that she lived in an apartment into which you could walk at any time. And good luck to you! But you hadn't the first idea where she ate, drank, spent any of those living hours of boredom that she'd bawled about that night in her husband's home.

Impatiently, he pitched the half-burned stub through

the window and hit the starting button. The shopping centre ahead was as good a place as any to start enquiries. From what he had seen and heard of Anne Felton, the liquor store best of all. His watch showed five minutes to two. It would still be open. He remembered that he had not eaten since the night before. A cup of coffee and a glass of orange juice had been all that a nervous stomach could stand that morning. This was the third day of the trial—Friday night might be the last. All the prosecution witnesses had been heard. Even if Galt decided to put Sullivan on the stand, the defence would be done to-morrow. Somehow, before then, he had to be sure of Felton. Certain that in spite of opposition, the juryman would dig in his heels for a verdict of "not guilty."

He parked outside a mock-Tudor shop-front with a door inscribed "The Butler's Pantry." It was an ill-advised attempt to combine Knightsbridge window dressing with the selling of liquor. There was a desk instead of a counter. Two walls were racked with bottles. Some crates peeped from behind a hardwood screen at the back of the store. Someone had adorned the desk with the plaster cast of a hand and a tortured strip of metal climbing from a cut glass base. Both were hideous. The whole place was in semi-darkness and carpeted with stained felt and a printed card broke the news.

WE ENCASH NO CHEQUES.

"May I help you, sir?" The accent was tasty—its owner as unlikely a spectacle as a dog playing a trombone. He had a sweep of yellow hair, with lighter streaks touched in. Underneath, a vaguely dissatisfied face. He swung slightly as he moved his elegance towards Steel.

"I hope so," Steel grinned ruefully. "I feel a bit of a fool," he confided. "I wanted to buy somebody a bottle

126

of Scotch—now I've forgotten the brand—"

"We have most, sir." The man pivoted with a flourish, graceful fingers demonstrating the whisky crates.

"The person I'm thinking of is a customer here." Steel spoke with assurance. He bent over the paper-wrapped bottles.

"If you gave me the gentleman's name, sir . . ."

"It's a woman, Mrs. Felton."

"Mrs. Felton!" The man skipped around the sibilants as though he thoroughly enjoyed it, "Oh yes, I know Mrs. Felton. The whisky of course, would *be* for Mrs. Felton."

It was the "of course" that did it for Steel. That and his knowledge of a queer's love of intrigue. He lowered his voice. "Look," he said confidentially, "there's not much point me telling you lies. You seem to me to be a man of understanding. I'm trying to locate Mrs. Felton." As the mouth began to make a prune, Steel hurried his words. "Not for any sinister reason, that, I promise you."

The man tossed back hair stiff with lacquer. As he touched the back of his neck, a heavy identity chain slid down his wrist. "How dull," he sighed.

Without knowing what the man was talking about, Steel smiled. "How do you mean, dull?"

"Well, I thought at *least* a sinister reason." The man was unpleasantly close. "You couldn't be that fabulous husband of hers, could you?"

The feeling that this freak had the answer gave Steel patience. "I could but I'm not. Just say 'interested party'. That covers it. Look, friend, I'm serious about the whisky. I'll buy it—you drink it. What I want to know is where I can run into Mrs. Felton—casually."

"You're not a policeman, are you?" one eye closed, the man had a sudden horror in his face.

"I'm not a policeman," Steel said patiently. "Just a

man who wants to meet a woman." He waited.

"Do you know her?" asked the man, tilting his head.

"By sight," said Steel. "And don't bother telling me that she lives over there." He jerked his head towards the Argyle Arms. "I know it." In the face of this sudden harshness, the other was passive—reproachful. Steel hardened his voice. "I want a pub—a park—anywhere you think she goes regularly in the afternoon." Just twice in his life, he'd seen her, he remembered. Getting out of a cab—in a patch of light at the bottom of the stairs. But he'd know her from a thousand.

Disapproval leaked from the corners of the man's full mouth. "It's hardly *my* fault if she gets herself into trouble, is it?" His voice was hopeful. He took a quick look at the door then confided. "When she first moved to the district, she used to be in here nearly every day. Always talking. Boring me with complaints about this husband of hers." He lifted a shoulder slightly. "I mean there are limits, *aren't* there? And one day—you know how they are sometimes—she was extremely rude to me. I've never *been* so insulted." He looked as if he might weep, then overcame it. "Now, we never converse. Never," he said a little regretfully.

"I know exactly what you mean," said Steel with sympathy. "It's tough. And it ties in with everything else I've heard about her. Now how about it—where do you think I could find her? She's not at home, I know that. Does she go for walks, anything like that?"

The man tittered, looking at his watch. He nodded delicately across the street to the house on the corner. "You might try there—any time after three. It's a bridge club but she uses it for a drink. Full of hideous old bags," the man said venomously. "You could try asking for her," he suggested.

"You've been a great help." Steel pulled a couple of

pounds from his wallet. "For the whisky I don't want."

The man moved a step nearer. The soft palm touched Steel's fingers as the money changed hands. "If you'd like to wait here for a while, you could. It might be gay." There was an unpleasant significance to the last word.

"Sure," said Steel. "I'll take a rain check on it." As the other looked blank Steel said: "Some other time. So long."

"G'bye," the other echoed sadly. "I hope you don't think me disloyal to Mrs. Felton. I always think men have a greater loyalty to one another than women, don't you, sir?" he added hopelessly.

"Without a doubt." Steel went out to the car.

He drove a quarter mile west to kill the time. Beyond shops and into a backwater of sanded roads, where the branches of the plane trees that lined them were strong and thick against the pale October sun. Rooks congregated noisily in the poplars beyond. Somewhere in the hedge was the clear sweet song of a blackbird. He sat there for a while, content. Till as always, the very peace of the spot filled him with discontent—a sense of loss—almost as if he had no right to be there.

He made a U turn, drove back and parked twenty yards up a side road, behind the house on the corner. It was a three storey villa with bow windows and toppling gables. From the car, he had an oblique view of the front and the porch, the short driveway. Unpruned larch trees blocked the light and air from the front of the house. Though the paintwork was fresh, the place had an air of having outlived its original purpose. At the back, a discoloured slat fence partially hid a garden discouraged by smoke and the hint of winter. Though it was still early afternoon, an overhead bulb burned pale in the porch. The only sign of life came from what would normally be the kitchen quarters. There, someone opened a door and the lid of a garbage can clattered.

It was difficult to know how he should get into the place. The ordinary London drinking club was a cinch to gatecrash. You breezed in behind a bright, expectant look at the bar, ignoring the receptionist and the member's book. It was a delicate gambit—unless the ease of manner was just right, you were likely to be shown the door. The alternative was the familiar nod and bold, indecipherable signature in the book. Presumably, a bridge club would yield to neither. A womens' club in a district like this— he saw them, middle-aged and dedicated.

He lit another cigarette, watching the clock. The club across the street filled him with sudden depression. It was a measure of Anne Felton's need to drink—and not to drink alone—that she chose a place like this to do it in.

A small car turned into the club driveway from the main road. Two women went up the steps to the porch, leaving the car under one of the larch trees. During the next ten minutes, a dozen more people arrived. All were women save for one tall man who moved at an amble as though late for an appointment.

Steel leaned back, resting his head against the top of the seat, eyes on the driving mirror. Squad cars were always prowling the neighbourhood. Sleek, black jobs with crews oily with false courtesy. "Excuse me, sir! May we have a word with you?" With three or four Suspected Persons Acts to cover their mistakes, police in high rental districts acted and then thought about it. Steel's story, in the event of a pull, was sound because true. He was about to go into that house on the corner and join a most respectable bridge club. And, thanks, officer for the interest and *of course* no hard feelings!

He was unable to get his mind off Felton. Right now, the juror would be walking round the car park at White

City, shepherded by a dozen cops. Steel saw the juror's face, faintly superior as if with some secret knowledge always. Before to-night was out, with luck, he might have the information he needed to change Felton's expression.

He straightened in his seat. A woman in a tan coat was turning into the club driveway. As she passed into the clear, beyond the trees, he recognized Anne Felton. She walked briskly, her long fair hair uncovered. He gave it a few minutes then locked the car and followed her.

The porch held a stand for umbrellas, three old copies of the telephone directory and a typewritten notice.

ALL ENQUIRIES—RING

He leaned on the bell push at the side of the door. The hall looked as if it might have been furnished by a committee of blind men on a rampage at an auction sale. Half as large as life, an olive-wood camel rammed its nose into a flower vase. Some decent-minded person had draped its hindquarters with a fringed shawl. Indifferent to its surroundings, a pendulum clock swung at the hours. He gave the bell a second shove. Somewhere in the interior a woman's voice called. In a moment, a maid appeared. She had a guileless face and a clean apron.

He took off his hat. "Good afternoon. Would it be possible for me to see the club secretary?"

"You mean Miss Pope?" She nodded. "Will you come in and take a seat, sir? I'll see if I can find Miss Pope for you. What name shall I say?"

"Steel." The name no longer mattered. He was in too deep, in case of trouble, to ever hope of getting out of it. He followed the maid into the hall and sat with his back to the camel.

The door behind him opened. Miss Pope was in her late forties, had blue-white hair and beautiful teeth. She

131

moved rather like a department store saleswomen—gliding as though on roller skates. "Mr. Steel?" she asked, showing her teeth.

He was quick on his feet. "You're the club secretary?"

She said "Yes," a little guardedly and waited.

He propped a hand unsteadily on the camel's slippery back. "I'm with one of our government departments over here." Let her make what she can out of that, he thought. "And I'm moving into the neighbourhood."

Her dark eyes were assessing him. He grinned, forcing their sympathy. "I've played bridge for most of my adult life—as a relaxation, of course. I'm not a gambler. And I'm a bad bridge player. But I'd sooner do without my whisky than my bridge." He looked at her hair and feet with frank admiration.

With an almost forgotten gesture, she touched the back of her neck. "Does that mean you want to join our club, Mr. Steel?"

Old or young, he told himself, if you gave them a reason for remembering that they were women, you had them on your side. "If that's possible. I'd be really grateful if you could help me, Miss Pope. A city like this can be pretty lonely for a newcomer."

In spite of the latent coquetry, she was still hesitant. "We are quite a small club, really. In fact, the membership list is almost full."

"I work most evenings," he urged. "It's as much for a place to sit with a pleasant drink in the afternoon as anything else." He saw the corners of her mouth turn down and thought, wrong answer.

"We do have a bar for members," she said slowly. "But we rather discourage the idea that this is anything else but a bridge club." The dark eyes were still sympathetic.

He ran a hand through his short black hair. "Miss Pope," he said impulsively. "I'll let you in on a secret.

If I have more than three drinks, I'm sailing." As he sensed her wavering, he insisted. "How do I join, Miss Pope?"

She sighed faintly but her face was pleasant. "Perhaps you'd better let me show you the club first." Hand on the still-firm flesh at her waist, he pushed her in front of him through the door.

What had been drawing and dining rooms was now the cardroom. Under green-shaded lights, fifteen women and one man were lost in their game. Nobody looked up as Steel and the secretary came in. Miss Pope touched his arm in the darkness.

"Some of them are very keen," she whispered. "Colonel Ogle's almost up to professional standard."

Steel had a closer look at Colonel Ogle. The army man had a fleshy nose that served as a toy for his fingers. A big man in his fifties, he had the remains of flashy good looks. White silk cuffs peeped from the well-cut jacket. Ogle was the sort of man Steel would not have trusted had he come, vouched for by twenty ministers of the Gospel. No doubt, thought Steel, in a clutch of old bats like these—blind to the niceties of the double shuffle, the colonel was on a good thing. In the green shaded light, he had the look of a stage Lucifer, and moved the cards with the deftness of an old boatrider.

Miss Pope's pressure on his arm again turned Steel's head. "Let's go into the other room," she whispered. They passed through the swinging door to a large room with three windows overlooking the garden. There were a dozen comfortable armchairs. On the walls, prints of Redoutée's roses. A bar cut across the back of the room. Anne Felton was being served a drink by a white-jacketed barman.

He had the impression that, suddenly, Miss Pope was trying to hurry him in and out. "This is the clubroom," she said. "The members use it while they're waiting to make up a table."

"What *she's* trying to tell you is that this isn't a gin mill!" Anne Felton swung herself round on the bar stool, her long blonde hair fanning over her eyebrow. She threw it back impatiently. Behind her, the barman was making gestures of hopelessness at Miss Pope. Ignoring Steel, the younger woman slid from the stool, the dark pleated skirt showing a length of firm leg." Not that there's much point in coming here for a drink. It's not only dull but expensive." She frowned, her blue eyes cloudy. "Tell me something, Miss Pope. Why do I *still* have to pay five shillings for brandy that I mix with ginger ale? What *is* the matter with ordinary three star brandy?"

The secretary's smile was forced. She moved to pass. "If you will excuse me, Mrs. Felton . . ."

Anne Felton turned and put her glass on the bar. "But *why?*" she insisted. Indifferently, she included Steel in the conversation. "You'll excuse a voice in protest, won't you?" Her mouth had a wry humour that he liked 'Especially if you're thinking of joining this Home for Distracted Matrons. You'll need cheap liquor. Tell me, sir." Her smile was warm and friendly. "Are you a brandy drinker?"

"It has been known," he admitted.

"Are you an American?" she asked curiously.

"Canadian."

"Canadian." She nodded. "Well, anyway, fellow-brandy-drinker, do you see good reason for paying five shillings for a *cognac de marque* that you don't even want?"

He shifted a shoulder, moulding his face to pleasantness yet unwilling to side with her openly. The barman took the pressure off. "I put three star on order, Miss Pope," he started. His nerves played hell with his grammar. "But it never come."

"Then see if you can get a bottle to go on with from the off-licence," instructed the secretary. She tried to by-pass Anne Felton again.

The blonde girl leaned against the back of her stool. Her eyes were hostile. She kept them on the secretary but spoke to the barman. "Don't bother, Arthur, they're closed. I know. Anything to do with drinking, then I'm the authority. Aren't I, Miss Pope?"

The secretary's patience was gone. "Yes, Mrs. Felton," she said simply.

For a second it seemed that Anne Felton had an answer. Then she picked up her glass. Her back, straight under its canopy of pale straw hair, was uncompromising. Steel went after Miss Pope, his sympathy ready. In the hall-way, she produced proposal forms from the bowels of the camel. "We usually ask for two members to sponsor all applications," she said. "But you are . . ." Forgetting the spectacles she wore, she was coquettish. "I almost said a foreigner—well, a *stranger*. If you fill in the form, I'll attend to the rest. The membership fee is two guineas."

He gave her his cheque. Address? Tongue in cheek, he wrote c/o Canada House.

"You wouldn't mind, would you, if I stayed on a little while this afternoon," he asked casually. "Just to get the feel of the place."

She put the papers away neatly and folded the camel's side before she answered. "You're a member, Mr. Steel. Do exactly as you wish, but there's something I should mention. I feel sure that you'll treat it with discretion. You noticed the girl in the bar. She's a member and there's nothing much we can do about it. When you know something of her history, it's easier, perhaps, to be more tolerant. She's charming at times, and attractive as I'm certain you noticed." Her look was uncomfortably knowledgeable. "But Mrs. Felton can be extremely embarrassing when she chooses." She opened the door for him. Suddenly she put a hand to her mouth. "How stupid of me! I completely forgot to ask what convention do you play, Mr. Steel?"

He managed a long, level look. "The Oshawa," he said with conviction.

"The Oshawa," she repeated slowly. "I don't think I know it. But then, it's probably Canadian. Never mind, we'll find *somebody* for you to play with."

He stood for a while in the darkened cardroom. Luck and keyhole peeping tactics had brought him thus far. But the woman on the other side of the door was no teenager to be overpowered with some hackneyed approach to a pick-up. With her background and her appearance, she would have been exposed to the brash and the subtle. But, somehow, he had to gain her confidence.

He'd have a big advantage. Anne Felton was a dis-satisfied woman. But dissatisfaction wasn't enough. A million women were dissatisfied with their husbands but they weren't ready to betray them. He wanted Anne to hate or at least be antagonistic. Instinctively, Steel felt she would talk—she'd talked to that queer in the liquor store. It helped a woman to convince herself that she had been wronged—humiliated, if she convinced others. If the urge were strong enough, it might include some stranger at a bar. Come to think of it, where else— save perhaps in a confessional box—did two strangers briefly share their personal tragedies as readily as in a bar! The danger factor was that liquor not only prompted soul-baring. Occasionally it screamed suspicion.

Steel moved round to the fourth table, the one nearest the pass door. He watched with mild admiration as Colonel Ogle leaned his elegant height towards his left-hand opponent, smiling courteous enquiry and dealing himself one off the bottom of the deck. The phoney gallantry of this dug-out rogue pointed a moral. The best cover for a hidden motive was a more obvious one. Let him convince Anne Felton of his indifference to her and—by implication—her troubled spirit and he created a challenge. He had a feeling that Anne was not good at ignoring challenges directed at herself.

"Game," said Colonel Ogle quickly and explored his nose. "And rubber, partner." He totted up the score, clicking commiseration for his opponents.

The woman on his left was arch. "It's hardly fair, Colonel. You're *much* too good for Mrs. Leswick and me." She leaned her large chest across the table, craning at the score. "That makes my share three pounds eighteen." She laughed heartily, her auxiliary chin bobbling. "What my husband is going to think if ever he looks at my cheque book . . . pay Colonel Ogle—pay Colonel Ogle . . ."

The bright blue eye was suddenly wary. "Were it the other way round, dear lady, I would feel even more disturbed."

Steel left them, pushing the felt-covered door. The dying sun tinged the room pink. Someone had thrown wood and coal on the fire. It crackled bravely with the restraint that a fire has in the sunlight. There were three empty stools at the bar. Steel took the one farthest from Anne Felton and concentrated his attention on the bottles on the shelves.

"A large scotch," he decided. "With ice and soda." An inner grumble reminded him of his hunger. "Is there any chance of getting something to eat?—a sandwich will do?" he asked.

"Ham, tongue, liver-sausage or cheese, sir."

From the way the barman spoke, Steel guessed that this would be the choice, three hundred and sixty-five days a year. "Cheese and ham. One of each," he ordered. He knifed mustard into the French rolls and ate greedily.

Without turning his head, he sensed that Anne Felton was looking at him. Her scent was a sharp sweetness that he sought to place, without success. Fair enough—the obvious scents were for women content to follow others. The more independence of mind that Anne Felton showed, the better he liked it.

He finished his drink and turned on the stool, elbows propped on the hard wood behind him. Out through the windows was a patch of lawn where a group of sparrows quarrelled over some titbit. In summer time, the members probably sat out there. He had a picture of Colonel Ogle, tipped backwards in a chair in the sun, shamming a doze with a handkerchief—a bandanna it would be—over his face. Underneath, an eye and ear alert for any sign of loot or danger. In the old days, not a single transatlantic liner, cruise ship, had been without its Colonel Ogle. Either alone or in a team, redolent of the Deep South or Poona, they attacked every smoke room and boat deck afloat with artistic effrontery. The war had dispersed them. A world cluttered with currency controls and treasury allowances held small room for international con men and card sharps. Here and there, one of the old school crawled out of semi-retirement, emerging in a place like this. Somewhere his rusty expertise was still good enough to handle impressionable matrons. Till later, there would be the inevitable tumble—scandal—and the Colonel would move on.

Recognition of the bogus brigade brought an unconscious smile to his face. It was a second before he realized that Anne Felton was talking to him.

"If the joke's that good, you ought to share it." She made a criticism of the words, rather than an appreciation. Steel was slow with his reply. "Yes," he said.

"Yes, *what?*" She looked up sharply.

"Just yes," he answered and went back to the sparrows on the lawn.

She tipped her glass, the heavy charm bracelet clinking down her wrist. Keeping her eyes on Steel as if he might elude her, she shoved the glass across the polished wood. Her laugh belonged to the brandy. It was a little too loud but determined.

"For God's sake, don't tell me we've acquired a character," she remarked to the room at large. With a lazy loop, she collected the fresh glass from behind her and cradled it in both hands.

"Arthur," she said over her shoulder, "I do believe our friend is a character. A whimsical, lovable character."

Steel resisted the urge to knock her on her can and he gave the barman his own glass. "Another scotch," Steel ordered quietly.

The barman was like a puppy with divided loyalty. Squirming, his eyes made the apology he had no courage to voice. Anne Felton leaned forward a little, her lips parted, the glass in one hand at an angle but controlled. "I don't think I like you," she said suddenly. This time she left no doubt whom she meant.

The deliberate insult rang up the memory of breaking glass, two nights ago, in Markham Square. The loud fierce anger of a drunken woman. One false move and she was gone for keeps. There was no time nor would there be opportunity to start all over again with this woman. So he sat the stool straight and smiled his best. "I guess that's for me," he said casually and looked her full in the face. Her eyes were the colour of Bristol glass in this light. A tiny pulse beat close to the smooth skin of her neck.

"If I did something to offend you . . ." he shrugged. "The times I get smacked down without knowing why!"

Her pale-pink mouth attracted him in a way he found disturbing. Like her husband she was too sure of herself. The wish to dominate her was strong yet Steel kept his grin an apology.

She continued to swing one leg that was long from the knee and fine at the ankle. "What's the matter with women that you find yourself so superior to them? Or is your disapproval for women who drink brandy in the afternoon?" Deliberately, she gulped her drink. The liquor was showing in what she said but not the manner in which she said it.

What he felt about women—her in particular—would do him no good in the telling. Sensing the need of the right answer, he took his time finding it. The barman had moved as far away as possible and stood polishing a glass with determined indifference.

There was a mirror, oval and in a gilt frame, hanging on the wall across the room. Anne Felton's face stared back at him. He watched the movement of her pale mouth in the mirror.

"A sensible answer, please, to a stupid question," she insisted.

There was a time when you knew if a woman was interested. And this was it. He turned so that he half-faced her. "What do you care?" he asked slowly. "What do you care about anything except behaving like a spoiled brat! I can only suppose it gives you a kick making complete strangers feel uncomfortable. But I've got news for you—I've got a hard hide." He made an arm and shifted the empty glass from her elbow. "For the record, I *like* women. It matters less to me if they crock themselves in the afternoon than if they're civil." He rapped with his ring finger on the bar. "A brandy and dry ginger for the lady," he ordered.

The risk was calculated. He watched, ready and

unsmiling as she hefted the glass in her right hand. The long, pink-tipped fingers tightened and then relaxed. As deliberate in her movement as Steel had been, she fished for a cigarette in her bag. When she found it, she waited till he thumbed a flame from his lighter. A little theatrically, she let the smoke dribble from a rounded mouth. Then she lifted her glass.

"Here's to the people who blow up jails," she said abstractedly.

He nodded, screwing up his eyes to shut out the memory the words held. "Here's to 'em, wherever and whoever they are," he agreed.

The ash on her cigarette had grown long. He leaned across, taking her wrist in his fingers, jolting the ash to the floor. Her skin was cool. As he lifted his glass to his mouth, her scent was faint on his finger-tips.

She shrugged in an odd way, one shoulder after another.

"Someone I know always used to say that. Do you find it irritating," she asked almost anxiously, "the way you're left with people's tricks of speech, long after they're gone?"

"I don't know that I've experienced it," he answered, "a husband?"

She pushed her hair back, jingling the charm bracelet. "Do I hear a note of sympathy—or is it just curiosity?" she asked. "Let me be curious," she said suddenly. "I'll guess what you do for a living." She squinted at the bottles behind the bar, as if they might hold inspiration. "You're a—what *are* Canadians? An ice hockey player—no?" A long swatch of fair hair fell over her eyes.

Corny, he thought. The Blonde Bombshell Routine that went out ten years ago. He looked at his watch. It was going on four.

"You look cute when you frown," he said. "But I'll

141

settle your doubt. I'm a clerk—an ordinary cypher clerk at Canada House and I work most nights. To-day I don't work—to-night I don't work." The rancour had gone from both their voices. Their stools had been moved closer. They sat in front of their drinks, shoulders almost touching with alcoholic camaraderie.

"Have you been married?" she asked mournfully. When he shook his head, she nodded thoughtfully. "One of the ones that got away—like my husband. Shall I tell you about my husband?" Some of the consonants she was slurring a little but she put words together with complete sense.

"Sure," he said, resisting the need to laugh in her face.

She looked at the gold band on her finger with vague interest.

"My husband's a creative artist. You know something— one creative artist with the need for freedom equals brandy at three in the afternoon. Have you ever thought of that as a reasonable equation?" It was a question lemon-sharp, without self-pity, but the laugh cracked a little.

Steel nodded. "If you want freedom, why get married! It's a contradiction in terms." A thousand times, he thought, he must have said *that!*

Twilight was making the garden bleak, the fire brighter, the room cosier. She eased one foot from its spike-heeled pump, curling her toes till they found the rung of the barstool. "You're a man—*you* give me the answer," she said flatly.

He stalled, uneasy as always with even the hint of fundamentals.

"How should I know?" he asked. He was having difficulty keeping his eyes from the slim, strong foot in its nylon sheath. "All men dislike surrendering their individuality—but I *can* understand a man wanting to

142

marry." He looked at her significantly.

"What about women?" She ignored the clumsy pass. "Or are they meant to like exchanging *their* individuality for a cookery book and the right to wash their lord and master's dirty socks?" She shushed him to silence with a finger. "Women are born to possess—men to resist it," she quoted. "That's the sort of talk I listened to for three years. But never again," she said with feeling. "Never again, thank God." She waved a hand at the barman. "A drink, Arthur. Two drinks."

That must be her fifth brandy since she'd been in the club, he thought. Possibly the sixth. There was no way of telling at what point she became unmanageable. It was a quarter to five, now. Any moment and she might leave the bar with a drinker's unpredictability He could ask her out to dinner. But you didn't offer a woman like this a meal—a stranger—without giving her reason to ask herself why.

As if determined to signpost the way for him, she spoke lazily. As much to herself as to him. "I've decided you're not a character after all. In fact, you're human. What's your name?" She used the fine lines round her eyes, the corners of her mouth, in a warm smile that looked meant.

Get close enough to her, he thought, and that smile would be hard to resist. "Steel," he said. "Gerry Steel."

She nibbled her bottom lip, giving his name consideration. "Mine's Anne Felton," she said at last.

He had the impression that she expected her words to mean something to him. She was watching him intently. Whatever else, the brandy hadn't reached her eyes. Blue-blue, they held their look steady. The sound of voices broke the deadlock. Craning his neck like a rooster, Colonel Ogle followed the three women into the bar. "Arthur!" he said loudly. "A strong pot of char for four! Over here, I think, don't you, ladies?" He whipped chairs

143

to the window with the speed of a conjuror. Settling his large behind in one, he sat gazing benevolently at the fire. Vaguely, he slapped the region of his pocket-book as if to ensure himself of its safety. "Delightful," he said vaguely. He inspected the room. As he saw Steel, the colonel's neck swelled slightly. Bending an ear to catch the whisper of the woman next to him, he worked feverishly at his nose.

Anne Felton was wriggling her free foot into its shoe. "In five minutes more, there'll be sixteen of them in here. It's more than I care to take, personally." She collected her handbag and gloves and stood perfectly still as Steel guided her arms into the coat sleeves. "I live a hundred yards away," she said over her shoulder. "If you'd like a cup of tea, I'll make you one." She turned round. The heels that she wore brought her eyes almost level with his. She smiled then gave that queer, lopsided shrug. "If you don't drink tea, goodbye. No doubt we'll meet again."

"There's nothing I'd like more," he said, hoping he wasn't putting too much enthusiasm into the words. He took his coat and followed her out under the furtive stares of the cardplayers. All the way down the drive, he had the uncomfortable feeling that Miss Pope was watching from a window. *Let* her watch, he thought. It didn't matter what she thought—what anyone thought. He had the old feeling of certainty—when you steered the puck round a couple of defence men, showering ice from your skates, and you *knew* you must score. Nothing was going to stop him now with Anne Felton. When he left her apartment, it would be with the information he wanted.

CHAPTER IX

At the Argyle Arms, the porters moved into the quiet speed of finger-snapping and door spinning that is reserved for favoured tenants. Anne only spoke once on the way up. A question that she asked, offhandedly, from behind her face mirror.

"Where do you live?"

The elevator operator was as impersonal as a ship's figurehead but Steel answered self-consciously. "I'm staying with friends. Till I find a place in this part of the world." His mistrust of people in uniforms extended to the man at the controls. This one had been on duty earlier in the afternoon. Steel avoided looking at him.

A red 4 flashed on the indicator board and the cage gates slid open. Blank faced, the man stood aside to let them out. "Thank you, Mrs. Felton," he said. As Steel passed, the man allowed himself the slightest smirk.

She led the way down the corridor and opened her front door, fumbling with the keys. There were those, he remembered, who faced with a couple of locks and keys, would inevitably make the wrong choice. That he would make better time at her front door with a strip of celluloid was no exaggeration. As the door closed, he noticed the short length of burglar chain and stout vertical bolts.

She hung his coat in a closet in the long hall and went through an open door into her bedroom. He had a glimpse of a wide bed in the shaded light—a bird worked in white on a black silk ground, thrown across it. He stood there for a second, enjoying the play of her arm as she brushed her hair. She turned. "Go into the drawing-room. It's the second door on your left."

He moved out of her sight and because of the inevitable need to be sure of a road of escape, opened the first door he came to. It was a kitchen, as sterile as an operating theatre with an expanse of monel metal and porcelain. Stark against the kitchen windows was the outline of an outside service stairway.

The second door opened a room warm and peaceful in the twilight. Red flickers from the electric logs in the grate stuck patches of lustre from the dark walnut furniture. What light there was came from an alcove at the far end of the room—an alcove shaped like a theatre box. He crossed to where the window made an arc fifteen feet long, and sat in a seat. Over the tops of houses behind the early winter tree skeletons, the homebound cars made the Outer Circle a loop of light. Beyond that was Regent's Park and the Zoo, dark now and free from human beings.

He sat in the warm obscurity, listening to the sound of crockery being handled in the kitchen. Even this room was faint with the scent she wore. He was a little disturbed by the ease with which his manoeuvres had succeeded. Had he been back in business as a thief, her friendliness would have queered the deal. You used to spend weeks, maybe, following a prospective victim, casing her home. Victims were less women than symbols representing X thousand dollars worth of jewellery. Then, once in a while, by some ironical chance, you met the woman socially—maybe you were even invited to her house for drinks, a meal. Casual courtesy that destroyed you and put her under the protection of a code as rigorous as that of the Bedouin tent-dwellers. He who gave shelter, food, was inviolate.

Anne Felton's jewellery was safe enough. All she had

at stake was her peace of mind. Possibly not even that. He needed a weapon with which to bludgeon her cocksure husband into surrender. With luck, she'd never know she'd provided it. Memory of Felton's smiling face— the fingers like skewers that grabbed suddenly—brought an ache to the nerves behind Steel's knee. But the pulse that beat in Anne Felton's neck, her quick vivid smile, took away some of the indignity of that moment in Felton's car.

Steel was uncertain of Anne's motive in asking him back to her apartment. With a woman like that, how could you tell. She lived in a world where convention mattered less than impulse. It might be no more than boredom. Ah well, boredom plus brandy had been known to produce unexpected results. He smiled in the dark. If he could get the information he wanted and at the same time clap the horns on the juryman, that would *really* be the business.

He walked over to the light switch and threw it. The room showed in soft perspective, the deep blue of the carpet reflected in the heavy velvet drapes. Gouache originals flanked the bracket lights on the cream walls. Books that were read were racked in shelves. It was incongruous that this ordered luxury should have the remotest connection with a whitewashed cell in Brixton Prison. At that second, Sullivan was locked behind a steel-lined door. Caged, in a sordid box, fifteen feet by eight. With the adjournment of court, the machinery of justice hung suspended until the next day. Judge, jury, lawyers—police and witnesses could divorce themselves from the trial and the issue. But never the man in the dock. If there had been some way in which Steel could have put Sullivan at ease. Let him sleep with the certainty of a verdict of "not guilty" under his pillow. There *was* no way. Nor was there any certainty until this woman and her husband were under his control.

147

He heard the sound of a tea trolley and pulled the drapes across the window, shutting out everything but the warm ease that surrounded him. The trolley was bright with silver. Anne handled the delicately patterned china with the indifference of someone who has never known any other. She wore the same dress. Its pleated length swirled slightly as she pushed the trolley in front of the fire.

"Do you like your tea strong?" she asked. Her hair was caught at her neck, making her younger. He took the cup she had poured and, still hungry, ate the sandwiches she handed across the tray.

"Gerry," she said suddenly. She held her cup in both hands, not drinking but using its warmth. Her eyes were curious. "It's a nice name. Would you mind if I called you Gerry?"

Smug with secret superiority, he spread a hand. He pushed his legs their length and considered the gloss on his shoes. "Why should *I* mind?" he asked with a grin. There was no hurry. She would talk when she was ready and he would help her. It needed only one idle remark and the same fury he had heard that night would show.

"This is a big place, you have," he said lazily. "How do you manage?"

She was up from her seat, standing in front of the fire at his feet, facing the mirror. He knew those women who needed a mirror to complement every gesture. She answered him now, staring into the framed glass without affectation. "I have a maid that I rarely see." She was indifferent, patting the loose hair at her neck. "She brings me tea in the morning and I never eat lunch here. By the time I get back she's usually gone." She moved her shoulders, one-two. "It's an arrangement I like." He nodded, eyes closed, indolent in the heat from the fire.

"Suppose you tell me what you really want, Mr. Steel, if that *is* your name." Their unexpectedness robbed the

words of meaning for a second. His mind grabbed frantically at some alternative explanation of what she was
saying. There was none. His answer sounded thin, without conviction. "I don't know what you mean." He
looked up at her.

"You don't?" In spite of the sarcasm, she had a look
of curiosity. Frankly bored with the tea, she walked over
to the drink cupboard. Ice chinked. She came back carrying a cut glass tumbler. She stood in front of the fire—
"Now just what are you?" she asked. "Some sort of
private detective?" She smiled without humour and
lifted her glass. "It's just possible my husband would be
that idiotic." She waited, without hostility, for his answer.

He fumbled with the denial. "No—I'm not a private
detective," he said, "I'm not a detective of any kind." It
was the best his shocked mind could do. Looking at her,
he knew that only the truth—or something pretty near
to it—would satisfy Anne. He tried to make his face
regretful, hiding his resentment.

"Then what?" she persisted. "A burglar?" She shook
the charms on her wrist. "This sort of thing?" she enquired.
"That's all you'd find." She sat on the edge of her armchair, mocking him. "Don't let this magnificent confidence of yours get out of control. It might make you
look foolish." She studied the pink on her nails for a
moment. "At a quarter to three I'm told that some
American—all right, *Canadian*—anyway somebody with
an accent like yours, has been making enquiries about me
in the off-licence. Just a half-hour later, you happen to
join a club where I'm known to go. Very smoothly, you
let yourself get invited to my flat. If you were in my place,
Mr. Steel—wouldn't *you* want to know why?"

In spite of the fury in his brain, his body stayed
relaxed. His legs still sprawled, his shoulders were balled
in the chair cushions. But having to look up at her

bothered him. Her mouth smiled but her amusement was *at* him. It had taken her sixty seconds to dynamite an edifice he had constructed with cunning and care.

"A moment ago you were so very sure of yourself," she pointed out. "Surely you must have *something* to say!"

He got to his feet, hating her doubly for being a woman and making a fool of him. Unconsciously, he went back to the pattern of movement that helped him to think. The cell-beat that an ex-con rarely loses. Five paces, turn. Five paces, turn.

Conscious of her in front of the fire, warm and assured, he aimed his words at the velvet drapes. "It isn't that 1 don't have anything to say. It's—well, the truth isn't easy, that's all." She gave him no help, just sat there waiting for him to go on. He must have been crazy, he thought, to have been so sure of that queer in the liquor store. He pictured the eager haste of the man, the more-than-feminine urge to shock with a share in a secret. Instinct told Steel that Sullivan's freedom depended on the next few minutes—if he could tell her enough of his plan to gain her sympathy.

With a mental salute to the Fate Sisters, he used her name for the first time. "You'll have to hear me out, Anne, if you want the truth. It isn't going to be easy for me. You're dead right—I pumped that queer in the liquor store, followed you into the Club. I was ready to follow you if it had taken me a hundred miles." His walk carried him from the fire to the alcove and back. "Simply because I had to . . ."

Two nights ago, he'd stood in the darkness and heard this woman silence her husband with an accusation. Only yesterday afternoon Steel had climbed into Felton's car, confident with the secret knowledge. And Felton had laughed at him. To freeze that laugh was going to take

Anne's help. Five minutes before, he'd been more certain of getting it.

She had taken his chair. Shoes off, her legs under her, she sat listening. As he paced up and down, her eyes followed him. "Stop it," she said suddenly. "Get yourself a drink or something, stop acting like a caged animal. It makes me nervous."

"Just how strong is your ethical sense?" he asked. He had her glass for a refill as well as one for himself. Behind the cupboard door he poured three fingers from each decanter.

She took her glass without comment. "You're talking in riddles. I'm not good at them."

"All right—how do you feel about the law? About people who get themselves arrested? Not *your* sort of arrests—" he tripped on the words—"the arrests your world condones. Stealing cops' helmets. Rigging traffic lights. Throwing Joe Blow into the fountain at Trafalgar Square. But real pinches." The lapse into the argot that matched the mood was done without thinking.

He was standing over her. She shifted her legs under her, balancing the glass on the arm of the chair. She smiled at him, full in the face. "Some women I know might have called the police by now—in my position. Is that an answer?" she asked mildly.

He shook his head. "Not without making fools of themselves, they wouldn't. What have I done?—joined a club where I met you—came back to your home, invited. You'll have to answer this question if you want me to make sense. How deeply do you identify yourself with the Haves against the Have-Nots? Are you with the man on the run or against him, for instance?"

She shrugged, deep in her chair. "I don't know that I have any feeling, one way or another. Not unless I'm personally involved. It's like politics or famines in China.

151

It's preposterous to expect me to take them seriously."
Her hand misjudged the distance from glass to chair arm
and brandy slopped on the carpet. She frowned. "But
you haven't answered my question—what's your interest
in me?" She put one slim finger to her mouth. "For God's
sake, not a poll-taker! I couldn't bear it if you were
one of those people who go round prying into the un-
speakable. '*Good*-afternoon'," she said in a mock bland
voice. " 'We're making a survey of the drinking habits
of grass-widows.' "

He shocked her because he knew it was time. "I'll
tell you what I am," he said. The cigarette he had lit
burnt till the hot smoke seared his fingers. He flipped it
behind the fake logs. "I'm a guy who's trying to save
somebody from doing ten years in Dartmoor. Whether or
not he deserves it's beside the point. I'm in a minority but
I happen to think he doesn't. That's why I started out to
follow you. Now—" he shrugged. "You know you're a
desirable woman. I ought to say that's a better reason.
It's a *good* one."

She was puzzled. "You don't make sense—what can
this have to do with me?" He made no answer but
watched the shake in his hands as if they belonged to
someone else.

"Drink your drink," she advised, "and get me
another. What you're saying is that you *are* a
criminal."

He stood behind the cupboard door. "Was," he corrected. "As far as people like you—the people who make
up Society—will let me use the past tense." He walked
back to her side. Her eyes were closed. "You could call
me technically honest at the moment. Just on the right
side of the jail walls. With the slightest shove, my position
could be altered." She opened her eyes. They were
without expression. "Your husband's on the jury in this

152

case, Anne. All he's got to say is 'not guilty' and my man goes free."

For a second, the blankness held in her face then she lowered her head into the crook of her forearm. Her back shook. He stood there uncertainly. He wasn't handling this right. Half-heartedly, he said her name once.

She sat up straight, wiping the laughter from her eyes. "I'm sorry," she said. "Blame it on the brandy." She moved her hand weakly, controlling the giggle in her voice with difficulty. "You can't realize how funny all this is to me." She pointed and he gave her her bag from the table. She dabbed with a tissue and put 'pink' on her mouth. "If it helps," she said, "I think you're nice. I like the things you do and the way you do them. But you haven't a hope. You were going to ask me to use my wifely wiles on Clive—on my husband, were you?"

Unwilling to believe in his own ascendancy any more—risk the chance of showing the wrong expression in eyes or in mouth, he turned away, making his voice hopeless. "How could I know? There was nothing I could offer a woman like you, that much I knew. I suppose I never got beyond the idea of telling you the truth and letting you make the decision. You've got to believe that I *was* going to tell you, Anne. Either you'd help, I thought, or—" he lifted his hands then let them fall. "Or you'd go to the police. Right now, you'd *have* a reason. A conspiracy to defeat the ends of justice, I guess they'd call it."

The upper softness of the arm she had behind her head was still tanned with the summer sun. "You found out all these things about me—about Clive. Didn't you know that we didn't live together?"

"Yes," he said. Maybe the truth but only that part of it that suited his purpose. No woman would want a witness to the scene she had staged that night in Markham

153

Square. "I knew all that. I've talked to your husband. He won't help." He lied now, "for all I know, he's told the police. It's a chance I had to take. I thought a guy like him might be a little more human. I was wrong."

She said nothing and he moved nearer her chair, seeking to convince her with the rush of words. He told her of Sullivan, of Kosky. Of the law's determination to railroad Sullivan for his share in the Braden Bullion Robbery.

When he had done, she took a cigarette and waited for him to light it. "I'll tell you something," she said. "I don't really care if your friend goes to jail or not. How *could* you expect it to concern me? You, I like." She put the ends of her fingers on the back of his hand. "What would you do if this man did get off?"

He scrubbed a dead butt into the ashtray. "Christ knows! It's the end of both sorts of world for me, in this country, anyhow. I'm no good as a thief. Take one guess what chance a guy like me has of making an honest living. People remember. People read." He forced a laugh. "There should be a law against it. I've even got to get out of my rooms on Saturday. Not because I don't pay my rent but because the witch who runs the place reads her newspapers."

She let the smoke drift between them. "Does that mean that you'll wander. Don't you have any ties at all?"

"None," he said definitely. "None that I can't pack in a suitcase."

She pitched her cigarette into the grate. "Whether you're cunning or lucky, I can't make up my mind. But I happen to be the one person who can give you Clive on a platter." The thought sent the laughter back into her throat. She leaned back, half-closing her eyes. "And I do have a reason for doing it. Gerry—do I still call you Gerry or is that an alias?"

154

He was behind her chair, his hands near her hair. "You might be able to give me another," she said softly.

Unhurriedly, he bent so that his mouth met hers. Her arms reached up, pulling his head down.

She walked the length of the corridor in front of him. As she went, she turned the lights off, one after another. For a moment, they stood close together in the darkened bedroom. Her fingers traced the outline of his face, the lines from nose to mouth. Her whispered words tightened his arms about her. Roughly, he pulled her down to the bed.

He woke to a pulse hammering at his temples and the befuddled resentment that comes from sleep at an unaccustomed time. An electric fire glowed on a white rug near the dressing table. The room was close with her scent. Hair fanned on the pillow beside him, she had her mouth half-open, breathing heavily. One arm, thrown in sleep, pinned the sheet to his chest. He pushed her arm away. It was still limp as he wriggled himself free from the heat of her body.

Watch and ring were still on the table at the head of the bed. Next to them, the blue pack of *Gauloises*. It was after nine o'clock. He lit a couple of the cigarettes and pulled the lobe of her ear, very gently. Only her eyes betrayed her waking. Then she moved a hand, an arm, slowly, to take the cigarette. "Hello," she said softly. Pungent smoke hid her face and she pushed a hand through it, impatiently. "You're the most civilized person, Gerry!" she said. Her eyes held steady and, for the moment, her mouth was tender.

A sort of indulgence, he thought—the tenderness shown to a disobedient child—an affectionate pat to a repentant pup. Behind was the threat of possession that irritated him. "Uh-huh," he said. The brandy on her breath was pretty strong. She punched a pillow, doubled it and put it under her head. Holding the sheet from one bare shoulder to the other with sudden modesty, she lifted herself in the bed. "You're funny," she said. "You're an absolute rogue and a rebel and you don't really care. I like it," she finished.

"There, you're way out of line," he answered. "The one sad thing in my life is that nobody recognizes my innate decency." He propped on an elbow and hoped that she wouldn't be whimsical. He had no time for whimsy— or romantic byplay. The jury box at the Old Bailey was clear in his mind and Felton in it.

"Don't be silly—deep down, you adore being the complete rascal." She stretched a hand that he avoided without being obvious. Her curled fingers were an inch from his arm. "Mr. Steel," she said softly. "The great rebel." The fingers moved and met round his wrist. "Suppose I said I liked you, not only because you're a rebel but because you're no different to anyone else underneath. Suppose I said you need someone like me to understand you?"

It was almost half-past nine. He still didn't have what he'd come for. He pushed his free hand through his dark cropped hair, kneading the tightness from his scalp. "I'd say that you were probably right," he conceded. "For limited reasons, I need you." His grin robbed the words of malice.

"Need me, just the same," she insisted, pulling his wrist so that the whole of his body followed. She took his face in her hands and kissed his mouth. "Still needed," she repeated when she had done.

The taste of her lips was good but treachery to a controlled remoteness that had been his for twenty years. With an uneasiness he was unable to explain, even to himself, he had always avoided the mouth of a woman. He kept his mind on Felton, speaking with as much

156

pleading as he could find. "You will help me, Anne?"

The telephone was on her side of the bed. She took the set and dialled a number. He heard the ringing at the other end then a man's voice. Anne sat up straight, shrugging the sheet round her shoulders. "Clive," she said with authority. "It's Anne. I want you to come over here, right away."

With the shock of hearing Felton's voice, Steel's body tensed. A hurried heart pumped blood to face and neck. He made a sound that was half-snarl, half-protest. She held the back of her hand to his lips, silencing him.

"I don't care *what* it is you were doing." She frowned at Steel, shaking her head. "It's important for both of us, Clive. Very important. You'd better come over here as quickly as you can." She was smiling as she put the receiver back on its rest. "He'll come," she said with satisfaction.

He was half-way out of the bed, awkward in his nakedness. "You goddam fool," he said bitterly. The resentment came with a rush. "Boy, what a pal *you* turned out to be! I'll tell you—you may be able to louse me up but you bet I'll fix you for it. *And* your husband." Careless of his words, he started pulling on his clothes.

"Gerry!" she called his name twice before he acknowledged it and turned his head. "You must be mad," she said quickly and reached across the bed, clawing at his hands. "Where are you going? I thought that's what you wanted me to do—I promise you," she insisted, "Clive will do whatever I tell him to do. He has to, Gerry."

He pulled away from her firmly. "What are you trying to do?" he asked. "Use me to show your husband what a knockout you really are? What's he supposed to do— come running back simply because you show him you can still get a man into your bed!" He reached for the light switch, jibing as she flinched. "Thirty-five," he guessed. "Another five years and the brandy bottle will have finished you as a woman." He still searched for a way in which to wound. "Help! The only person you'd ever help would be yourself."

He bent over to knot the laces in his shoes. He could hear the muffled sniffling as she tried to stop it. He made a careful loop in his tie then turned from the mirror. "For Crissakes, spare me the tears," he said. "Save them for your husband and let me out of here before I put your head through that window."

Shocked disbelief in her voice, she shook her head. "I don't believe it," she said. "You couldn't be such a bastard. What woman did that to you, Gerry?" She wondered. "I meant every word of what I said to you. What do motives matter. What does *anything* matter?" She hid her face suddenly, pushing his hand away.

He sat beside her on the bed, ashamed of the rage to wound. The lack of reason that always forced him to attack even when uncertain of cause. Of *course* treachery on her part was incredible. She'd merely acted with a stupidity that she probably didn't recognize. His words came grudgingly but loud enough for her to hear. "I'm sorry, Anne. Half the time, I don't seem to know what I'm saying."

She screwed her head round, using the sheet to dab her reddened eyes. "These *bloody* tears," she complained. "I don't like them any more than you do. Please tell me," she urged. "Why mustn't Clive come here?" There was something defenceless about the odd little shrug, now done with bared shoulders. "I'll call him and tell him, no," she said suddenly.

They sat close together, listening to the insistent double ring at the other end of the line. After a few minutes, he took the receiver from her hand and replaced it. "No matter," he said quietly. "Just don't answer when he

158

comes. You've got to keep out of all this, don't you see it, Anne? I don't care *what* kind of argument you'd use. If your husband comes here"—he covered the disordered bed, their intimacy—"he'll see you in hell first. It's only natural. I don't care *what* terms you're on—you're still his wife. And don't fool yourself—this is jail bait we're playing with. One false move and we *all* finish up where Sullivan is." He put his cheek next to hers. "The Scarlet Pimpernel was in a book, Anne. This is rough stuff."

She nodded. "Then how . . ."

He stopped her. "You only force a man with a threat that you can make good. Has Clive ever been in the pokey himself?"

Her mouth was derisive. "Clive? He's been everything. Judge, prisoner and jury. But up to now, always in his head. "No," she said finally.

"But he could have been?" urged Steel.

"Still can," she said.

"And that's the answer. That's why he's bound to do whatever you say?"

"Yes."

"Then you've got to tell me why." He was definite. "And when I leave here to-night, I'm going to see him."

"Don't go," she whispered. "Not yet. I don't want to be here alone when he comes."

Because he suddenly wanted to, he held her close to him. "I won't," he promised and switched off the light. Together, they sat in the darkness and waited.

CHAPTER X

TRYING to forget her nearness, he encouraged her to talk about Felton. She did so readily—almost as if she strengthened her position by sharing the facts with Steel. With a deadly memory that he noted, she remembered dates and amounts covering her husband's work outside the country, from Rome to Paris and back. Every job Felton had done for a foreign studio, every nickel he had failed to declare.

It was impossible in the dim bedroom for Steel to see the expression in Anne's eyes but her voice was wintry. "Make sure that Clive understands that you'll tell the Authorities if he doesn't do exactly what you want, Gerry."

With a thief's discrimination, the idea of extortion was distasteful to him. He rationalized. The whole thing was a chapter that after to-night would be dead. Felton an accidental victim. He bore the guy no animosity, Steel told himself. The quick humiliation of the moment in the juryman's car gave him the lie.

"I'll make sure," he promised. She nodded her satisfaction.

Christ, how she hated. She wasn't the kind to promote as an enemy he thought. Now she knew Felton was going to be fixed the man would be in worse shape than ever. Ah well, no reason why Steel couldn't forget the pair of them as soon as the verdict was returned. Half his brain hold him that. The other half pushed his fingers through the hair at her neck.

Count of the time had gone when the doorbell rang sharply, twice. He sat up straighter on the bed, tightening his grip on her shoulders. Fifty memories sharpened his ears to the slightest sound. Memories of an insistent knock at the street door while, inside, he waited for the cops to either crash in or go. Memories of the unoccupied flat where you emptied a jewel case into your pocket to the shock of a bell rung unexpectedly by some casual caller.

The bell sounded again then someone lifted the door-knocker and let it fall, tentatively. Steel kicked off his shoes and tipped the length of the hallway. He put his weight against the door, carefully, from the inside. Then moved the bolts. They went home easily and without noise. He had one ear against the door which was acting as a sounding board. From outside gloved fingers raised the flap of the mail box. The metal squealed protest. Light slitted the carpet at Steel's feet and he pushed his back hard against the wall.

Holding the flap open, Felton put his mouth to it, his voice distorted as if he were calling up a chimney. "Anne! Anne!"

The flat was completely silent. Had Steel pressed down suddenly, he could have trapped Felton's fingers in the slit in the door. Only an inch of wood separated the pair.

"I know you're in," called the juryman. "They told me downstairs." The strong spring snapped the flap shut as Felton let it go. Holding the door by the handle, he rattled it. "Don't be a bloody fool," he shouted into the door crack. The wood strained as the man put his shoulder to it. A couple of times, he slapped the door with the flat of his hand then the passageway outside was quiet.

Steel went back to the bedroom. In the fireglow, her hair was dark against the pillow. A pyjama top was pulled round her shoulders. He sat down beside her.

"He's gone," she whispered, her fingers going inside

161

his jacket. "He's gone, hasn't he?"

He moved his head from side to side. "Downstairs, he's gone. In a minute, that 'phone's going to ring. Whatever you do, don't answer it."

The instrument sounded as he spoke. It rang for two or three minutes, then stopped. "Now he'll be back with the porter," said Steel. "Has he got keys to this place?"

"The head porter has a spare set in his desk," she answered. "In case of fire or burglary."

Voices outside the front door sent Steel back there. He watched as first one key then the second was turned. Held by the bolts, the door was immovable.

"Turn both keys, man," said Felton unsteadily. "When I put my weight against the door, push!" The door merely creaked.

The porter's voice sounded, pompous with technical knowledge. "There must be somebody in there sir. This 'ere door's being 'eld on the bolts."

"Brilliant," said Felton.

There was a clink as keys were returned to a ring. Then the porter's voice again. "The 'ead porter's not on, sir. But I could 'phone the police if you liked."

With the suggestion, Steel's brain tried to put his legs in motion. He saw the whole deal. The ponderous hammering as the law demanded to know what was going on in there. The inevitable scene. The explanations that would convince nobody. He stayed where he was.

Felton reacted with sarcasm. "That's an even more brilliant suggestion. It could be that my wife has fallen asleep. In which case the police seem superfluous. I'll 'phone her later on."

The porter was obviously pouching a coin. "Thanks very much, sir. Good night, sir."

Once more, the passageway outside was quiet. Steel went down on his knees and pulled away the mat. Flat

on his side, he peered through the clearance at the bottom
of the door. He turned his head so that he could check the
other angle. There was nobody out there, either in front
or to either side of the door. He put the mat back and
dusted his hands.

In the bedroom, he closed the door and switched on
the light. "Now he's gone," he told her. "Probably headed
back for Markham Square. You'll have him on the 'phone
every ten minutes till he gets sick of it." He touched her
cheek. "I've got to go, lovey. I'll take the back way out.
Every one on this floor is probably hiding behind their
front door, waiting for someone to come out of here."

"How about if I went out?" she suggested. "Then you
could follow later?"

He picked up his cigarettes from the bed-table. "That'd
make no difference. These porters are going to remember
me." He looked down at her. "Five gets you fifty that
they know I'm still up here. If nobody sees me go, so
much the better. How about those steps from the kitchen.
Are they lit at the bottom?"

She caught her lower lip, frowning. "I don't think so—
certainly not up here."

"Where does it finish—out in the open or in some hole
in the ground with one of the porters sitting beside it?"

"In the open," she answered. "There's the staircase
and a sort of lift that the tradesmen are meant to use for
deliveries. Why do you have to go now?" She asked
suddenly. "There's nobody likely to be on duty at six
in the morning downstairs. You could slip out then."

He cocked his head. "At six in the morning, I want to
have Felton screwed in a little tight knot. One way or
another, before I go to bed to-night, I mean to be sure."

She gave him no further argument "You'll have to be
careful, Gerry. There are lights outside all the garages.
And the only way out is past the front lodge."

163

There'd be walls he could climb wouldn't there, he asked himself with irritation. He was anxious to be gone, now. Sick of the heaviness of this room and the need of this woman.

"I'll manage," he assured her.

"Will you ring me just as soon as you've seen Clive?" she asked.

Ring me, see me, tell me, he told himself. Would he never meet a woman who wouldn't, sooner or later, stake claims on everything that he held personal. He put his fingers through her hair again. "I'll ring you just as soon as . . ." Whether they ever saw one another again after the verdict depended on so many things. How little she showed insistence on sharing his life, perhaps, most of all.

"How will I know that it's you ringing?" She put her hand to her head, imprisoning his fingers in hers. "You said not to answer the 'phone because of Clive."

"I'll let it ring three times my end then hang up. I'll do that twice. The third time, answer." He took away his hand.

She wanted to go on. "I know so little about you, Gerry. I don't even know where you live." She made it sound monstrous.

"Till this case is over, the less you know about me the better," he told her. He grinned. "If I don't 'phone, I'll either be dead or in the lock-up. I'd be no good to you in either case." He kissed her now with finality and a certain amount of compunction. The whole goddam world was cluttered up with "if onlys." He shut the bedroom door on one of them.

With its gleam of metal and porcelain, the kitchen gave its own faint light. Through the window in the back door, he saw the iron stairway as it coiled round the service elevator shaft. Outside was dark save where from some of the kitchens above and below light leaked out into twisted shadows. Way down, at ground level, the night hid everything from the walls of the block to the garages, fifty yards to the rear. A medium-powered bulb hung in a case over each garage.

He pulled back both bolts, taking time because it was habit. Then turned the heavy mortise lock. Gripping the handle, he opened the door an inch. Unmistakeable, the sound of leather on iron came from underneath him. Hugging the shaft to avoid the lighted back doors, a man was climbing the stairs. He was thirty feet below. As he moved into the next yellow patch, Steel recognized Felton's light grey coat.

Without haste, Steel turned the key in the lock and pushed back the bolts. Then he climbed into the metal sink. Through the large window, he had an oblique view of the iron stairway and the landing outside. A faucet was dripping water into his shoe. He moved the foot to the draining board. Felton's head was showing clearly now. Lips pursed as though whistling, he climbed the last few steps then, very gently, the handle turned on the door, the door itself creaked. From the landing outside, it would be just possible for Felton to reach the half-open window over Steel's head. If it could be pulled down, a chancy step from the iron railing would land him beside Steel in the sink.

As the fingers from outside strained at the sash, Steel pulled his body behind the curtains. With one hand, he held the bottom of the window pane firmly. After a moment, the fingers disappeared. There was a scraping outside as Felton scrambled back to safety.

Showing no more concern than he would have done for a jammed window, Felton walked to the back door. Nose flattened against the glass panel, he stared into the kitchen. Baffled, he leant his shoulders on the elevator shaft and considered the windows on each side of them.

The propped leg, the one Felton had mangled, was giving Steel trouble. He pulled it down and lowered his weight till his buttocks hit the edge of the sink. Felton looked set for the night—as if determined on solving his wife's silence, personally. Steel wanted him back at Markham Square, snug and secure behind his own front door. A taut balloon, ready for puncturing.

Centering senses in his fingertips, Steel groped behind him till his hand touched metal. He swivelled his head to look. At chin level, a shelf held a row of aluminium pots. He lifted one of the lids gingerly. He kept his eye on Felton, silhouetted in the door panel. A cigarette glowed out there. The juryman seemed to be settling down. Steel hoisted himself up till his chest touched the open window. With three careful fingers, he pushed out the metal lid.

Two floors below, it bounded on the iron treads and careered off into the darkness. The *thup* as it hit a flower bed below was almost inaudible. Felton's shoulders hunched with the sound and his hands grabbed at the balustrade. Very carefully, he started tiptoeing down to the lower floors. Wasting no time, Steel went to the back door. The stone-coloured coat showed briefly as it moved into a patch of light, a couple of floors below.

Steel pushed his lighter flame into drawers—a cupboard—till he found what he was looking for. A plastic bag that he filled from a flour bin and shoved deep in the pocket of his storm-coat. Then he slid back the bolts, unlocked the door and slipped out to the landing. Once more, he rammed home the heavy mortise lock, this time from the outside. Should Felton start back up the stairway, it would be easy to climb to the roof. The man had no key to the kitchen door. For a moment, Steel played with the idea of using the service elevator in some way. Thought of the noise stopped him. At this hour of the night, an alarmed tenant could have the neighbourhood overrun with cops in almost as little time as it took to dial 999. Only a block away, his car stood, unattended.

He gave it five minutes, checking his watch in the glow of his cigarette. The only sign of life from beneath came from kitchens where meals were being cleared away. He started down the stairs. He would be in safety at least till he reached the second floor with its light. The kitchen door showed ajar. Six feet above, he watched as a woman manoeuvred a garbage pail to the landing then went inside. As he went past the lighted window, he ducked his head. There was another danger spot, one storey down. But there, a maid sat with her head cradled against a radio. The last twelve treads, he took at a run.

He was on a patch of grass, soggy with lack of sun. Over on his left, a paved way curved from the garages to the front of the block. The building showed brick-red at the corner, in the light of an overhead arc.

Maybe Felton had left his car somewhere near. There was no reason why the man shouldn't pound on his wife's back door as well as the front. But the space in front of the garages was empty.

On both sides, brick walls stretched to a copse at the end of the grounds. Beyond the far wall, Steel's own car was parked. He walked round the iron spider work and into a patch of deep shadow. He heard a grunt then felt sharp agony as metal bit into his shoulder. It was too dark to see Felton but Steel knew as the second blow came. This time, Steel took the brunt on his upper arm, content to gain time. Felton's left hand grabbed, taking a lucky hold on the collar of the storm-coat. Steel let himself sag, wrestling at his pocket. The strap on the collar was cutting into his throat, blocking his windpipe. The juryman struck savagely, keeping the blows aimed at body and limbs, ignoring Steel's unprotected head.

To break a bone, thought Steel. He was down now,

nails digging into the damp turf. Desperately, he pulled
the bag free with the other hand, pumping the open end
into Felton's face. Blinded by the flour, the juryman tore
at his eyes with both hands. A tyre lever dropped at his
side. In grotesque parody of a child's game, Felton was
stumbling about, hands outstretched before him. Steel
scrambled up and moved in between the man's spread
arms. As hard as he could, he belted Felton between the
eyes. Then another punch, swung on the end of an arc
and into the man's belly. A mask of flour, gasping for
breath, Felton fell to his knees. He wavered, grunting pain
then pitched forward.

Steel moved to the shadow of the ironwork and stayed
there till the figure on the ground moved. Felton rolled
over a couple of times then spread his arms and retched.
Very shakily, he got to his feet, and wiped his face free.
For a while, he leaned against the brickwork, holding his
stomach, then disappeared round the lighted end of
the block.

Steel's shoulder hurt where the metal rod had bitten
into the bone. As he ran for the wall, he felt under his
shirt where blood gummed it to the flesh. Over the wall
and through the dead leaves, thick under the larches. He
stopped on the bridge club side of the palings. On the
other side of the fence, a couple went by, their conversation dreary with banalities. He climbed the fence and went
over to his car.

As he passed the apartment block, he looked for signs of
Felton. The driveway was deserted. Only in the shadow of
the lighted portico, the doorman was jigging a little, to
offset the growing cold.

He cut through to Maida Vale, along the canal road to
the railroad viaduct and into the park. As he turned east
to the King's Road, the clock under the town hall showed
almost eleven. He drove slowly, past the crowded espresso

bars filled with bearded men and greasy haired women crouching in duffle coats. Here and there, groups of Teddy Boys shoved improbable shoulders in the way of the theatre crowds, challenging the police patrols.

A space showed at the bottom of Markham Square. He took the Zephyr in and cut the lights. At the far end of the square, Felton's car was standing in front of his house. The blood had caked on Steel's neck muscles. The wound pulled raw as he put his hand to it. He made a pad with a handkerchief. There was no other break in his skin but a dozen aches were dull, now, in his arms, his legs. He fished under the dashboard till he found the short blackjack. Leather plaited round a lead base. With Felton, it was better to be prepared.

He locked the car and walked round to the far side of the square, in the shade of the bush and hugging the railings. The light over Felton's front door was out but movement showed through the gap in the curtains. There was no point in waiting. He pulled the gate shut after him and knocked at the street door, twice. Then he stepped back, just out of range of the longest arm. Though the hall stayed in darkness, the light came on over his head. He made no move as the door opened slightly.

Felton looked as solid in a bathrobe as in a suit. A strip of plaster divided his eyebrows. As Steel cocked his head slightly, Felton recognized him. "What do *you* want?" he asked.

Steel answered, "The same as last time, Felton, I want to talk."

The juryman flipped both the hall switches, leaving Steel in shadow but lighting the hall. Without a word, he held the door open. Then it clicked shut and the two men stood in silence. Unhurriedly, Felton put a hand to Steel's collar. The strap, where the juryman had gripped

169

it earlier, hung on a few stitches. He let it fall. "I'll take your coat, shall I?" he asked quietly.

Steel turned his back deliberately, nerves protesting as the coat slipped down his arms to the elbows. *Now*, he told himself, *now* it'll come—the swift pinioning jerk, then the probe of the other's strong fingers.

Felton let the coat fall to the chair and hitched the cord of his robe. "In here." He jerked his head at the open door. A foot slid a chair in Steel's direction, then Felton pulled the curtains shut tight. He sat on the end of the sofa and waited. Purple mouses had started to puff the juryman's eyes. Shoulders balled under the terry-towelling, he looked like some useful middleweight rather than a scriptwriter.

The dead weight of the blackjack in his pocket gave Steel back a little of his confidence. But not quite enough. Felton was beaten physically in a way that must still hurt—he'd been cuckolded—yet he still seemed to have the initiative. He sat, swinging one leg across the other in the manner of someone who gives time but is not willing to lose any.

"Well?" Felton said. "You haven't come here to ask after my health. I take it we're going to discuss a number of things." He flexed the fingers of his right hand, touching the strip of plaster between his eyes. "And you don't see me at my best. A little tired," he jibed. "Perhaps you'd better start talking . . ."

Steel's certainty of manner reached no further than his words. He eased himself into the chair. Physical fear of the other soured his stomach. "It's a straight deal now," he said. "I'll keep my mouth shut for Sullivan's freedom."

"Keep your mouth shut," Felton repeated thoughtfully. "About what, for example? My wife's readiness to climb into bed with you?" His feet, bare under pyjama trousers, were small for a man of his size. He took his weight on them delicately, as if testing his spring. "Are you naive enough to imagine that I don't know her by now?" He reached for the cigarette box and blew smoke at Steel. "My wife's been a tramp for years," he said flatly. "Assistant camera men, any of my friends that she fancied. You . . ." He shrugged. "It isn't a pretty picture but it's hardly blackmail material."

Always this refusal to acknowledge force, thought Steel, hating the other man's composure. He chose words that would jolt. "How about tax evasion—would that be blackmail material?"

Felton's laugh just failed complete ease and he avoided looking at Steel for a second. "Don't tell me she trotted out that pipedream! Anne's been hawking it round for months. Selling it to anyone who'd listen. It's part of the line, chum. The complete shit of a husband—impossible and dishonest as well." He pitched the cigarette at the ashtray. Then he stood up. "If that's as far as it goes, I'll tell you what I'm going to do. I'm going to leave you so that you won't feel like getting out of bed for a month, to start with." He moved a couple of easy steps nearer. "And then make sure that your friend goes down. It's a toss-up which of the two I found more objectionable, Kosky or Sullivan. But meeting you decided me."

Steel was out of the chair with a quick movement. He put his back against the wall, the leather-covered lead in his hand. "You bland bastard," he said viciously. "It isn't going to be like that at all." He pulled the paper Anne had given him from his pocket. "Not for a nickel's worth, it isn't. I've got every date—the number of every cheque you were paid with. Rome as well as Paris." He returned the paper. "I could phone the tax 'people from a hospital bed as well as from anywhere else."

Felton was back on the sofa. He looked at Steel, shading swollen eyes against the light that was between them. "Sit down," he said suddenly, "You know there isn't going to be any need for you to use that thing in your hand." His voice rose and Steel saw that the man's hands were shaking. "Christ, what a crew," Felton said bitterly.

Steel pocketed the lead and came over to the sofa. Fifty times, the past few days, he'd told himself that this would be the moment. Now he knew that almost any other way would have been better. Suddenly, he wanted to tell Felton, forget it. There was a sense of shame. As if your best friend had caught you with your hand in a blind man's pocket. Seen you and looked the other way.

"I'm no extortionist, Felton," he said slowly. "Once this case is over, I want nothing from you. Nothing that's yours," he said with emphasis. "But I intend to make sure that Sullivan goes free. You tell me this—what does the jury think now? About the case. Sullivan."

Felton's head was back on the sofa. He closed his eyes. "Well—this is it," he said at last. He sounded tired—as if knowledge of his wife's double betrayal had made him unequal to Steel. "We sit there, listening to two stories, both sides claiming the facts." He opened his eyes again, they were almost lost in the swollen flesh. "Don't you *know* what ordinary people think—that the police wouldn't have put him there if he hadn't done *something*?"

"I know it," Steel answered.

"Well they're ordinary people, this jury," said Felton. "Just an audience for Clarke and Trelawney. It's like somebody listening to an opera in Russian. You admire the production but enough is enough." He leaned forward, massaging his stomach. "A bolo punch," he said sourly. He straightened up. "Eleven of us are going to be for finding your friend guilty."

"Eleven won't be enough," Steel said. "And remember this. You're going to be in that court—even if I have to carry you there. Blind, even. That's just in case you had ideas of weaseling out, with a doctor's certificate, for example. And some sad tale to me about how it wasn't your fault. I have news for you—at this stage, the judge would go on with that trial with eleven—maybe ten jurors. Tomorrow, you're going to be there, ready to sit to a deadlock."

Felton managed a yawn, stretching. "As much as anything, I'd like to know how to fit into all this. Not that business with Sullivan, but how it all started . . ."

"I was misunderstood," Steel told him. "And my mother dropped me on my head every day from the age of six months. It doesn't help. Just one thing, Felton. In case you're getting morally superior about all this, you'd better remember just why I'm here."

Felton's hand acknowledged the cut. "Two rogues, in other words. I take it you've never been married to a woman with six times as much money as you have yourself?" He pulled the flesh down from his eyes, looking into the mirror. "But then you'd say your friend had as much justification for whatever he's supposed to have done." He turned round, smiling but the smile never went farther than his lips. "That's about covered everything, hasn't it? A rogues' agreement. Your silence against mine when my colleagues say guilty."

Steel followed the other to his feet. "You can forget about me the moment Sullivan walks the street," he promised. "Nobody can force you to say guilty, Felton. If you do . . ." He chopped with his hand as though at a block of wood. "But you won't . . ."

Neither man made a move to push out a hand. They went out to the hall. "Will you mind if I say something rather personal?" said Felton.

Steel picked up his coat from the chair. "We know one another well enough."

The juryman held his street door ajar. "Just this. Anne doesn't give up very easily. I'll be intrigued to see how you get her out of your life when the time comes."

The crushed bone was agony as Steel lifted arms into his storm-coat. "I wish all my troubles were as worrying."

Felton thumbed the hall switch. "There I can say I hope so. I certainly hope so." One last time he managed a smile that was disquieting.

CHAPTER XI

THE square was deserted. A couple of times on his way to the car, Steel turned round to look at the house. It was in complete darkness. He sat for a while in the car, unwilling to believe that at last it was done. He might well have had a signed release for Sullivan in his pocket. He wanted to laugh, rather weakly. Years now, with resentful cops waiting for one chance to pin something on Sullivan. A room in the house facing St. James' Park where someone at the Director of Public Prosecutions prepared a brief, certain of the issue. The whole parade of justice-expediency made a sucker of by a couple of words from a tax-dodger called to jury service.

He switched on the motor and pulled the Zephyr into the King's Road. At the back of Peter Jones, he stopped at the 'phone booth. The wish to call Sheila was strong. It wasn't just the desire to tell her that Sullivan was safe. He wanted to demonstrate what she seemed to deny. That to a man faced with jail, unscrupulousness was of more use than a pious belief in faith, hope and charity. But now, more than ever, the need was for secrecy.

In the booth, he called Anne's number. She answered the third time. "It's me," he said quickly. "Everything's all right. How about your end?"

"The same," she answered. "You woke me up." She yawned, making a grumbling sound in her throat. "I heard nothing otherwise. Where are you?"

"In bed," he lied. "Can I call you about six tomorrow?"

She made an endearment of her voice. "Can you? Try *not* calling me, Gerry!"

"What?" he said impatiently.

"Love me?"

Tomorrow was another day and not till he heard Sullivan discharged would Steel rest. "Sure," he said into the mouthpiece. "In a year's time, baby, maybe we'll both mean it." He hung up.

He drove back and parked, then went up to his rooms without thought for the darkened doorways, the still line of cars. The uncertainty and fear of the last three days were almost done. He'd put his liberty in jeopardy and like a mouse that scuttles a dozen feet from refuge to refuge, behind some sleeping cat, he had the sense of living again. Later, perhaps, time would blur all memory of danger, leaving him smug in his own cleverness. But till then, he wanted to forget the details and remember one thing—Sullivan was safe.

Upstairs, he took the 'phone on impulse though it was well after eleven. He called the Chiswick number and Sheila answered. "It's me—Gerry," he said. At the tone of her voice, he added, "What's the matter?" For weeks now, imagination had been making a fool of his judgment. People's voices—their faces seemed to hold ill-omen. Most of the time, he'd been wrong but the compulsion was beyond his control. There was *something* wrong with

Sheila, he told himself. She still hadn't answered. "What's the matter?" he asked again.

"Nothing's the matter," she said at last. "It's just that it's late and I was going to bed."

Only half-convinced, he sought further assurance. "There's nothing wrong with Danny, is there?" A dozen times in jail, Steel had heard the pad of the night patrol turn into a frantic scurry—then the alarm bell sounded. Doors crashed open and the screws cut down some poor bastard hanging from his window. It was too easy, with the certainty of years of imprisonment. A strip torn from the sheet—one end knotted to the bars, the other round your neck. The stool you stood on, kicked away with the last hopelessness. It was a less rapid death than the gallows. Unless the patrol found you in time, you strangled instead of having your neck broken. "Danny's all right, isn't he?" He tried to keep his voice calm.

"Yes." Her weariness made the word almost inaudible. "They let me talk to him for almost half an hour before they took him to Brixton."

"You go to bed," he said quickly. "Tomorrow night you won't be sleeping alone." He tried for some assurance that he might give with safety. "Sheila—remember what I'm telling you. Danny's going to be all right!"

"I'll remember," she said. Then—"Good night, Gerry."

"Good night," he said and waited for the line to go dead.

Her voice sounded again. "Gerry—Galt phoned this afternoon. He says the case is going to finish tomorrow."

"What do you think I'm telling you?" he said impatiently. "What of it?"

"Nothing," she answered. "Only that Alan wants to come to court."

"Great," he tried to smile his way to the room where she'd be sitting. "That'll be one more I have to buy champagne for. See you at ten-thirty, honey. Good night," he said again and put the receiver back on its rest.

Hunger was nothing more than a void to be filled anyhow. He did it with a can of frankfurters and a blackened banana that he found in a paper sack. Then he kicked off his clothes and stood naked in the bathroom. The wound on his shoulder had caked. He soaked off the padded handkerchief and poured iodine into the cut. He strapped a clean dressing on his shoulder with adhesive tape. Gingerly, he let himself down in the steaming bath and eased the aches in his body and limbs. It was nearly one when he set the alarm for seven that morning. He had to be moving early.

He awoke unwillingly and silenced the clatter of the clock. Every movement he made hurt. He walked stiffly to the window. Friday had come in with a low grey sky just starting to make itself seen. The street lamps were still lit. He opened the French windows and stood on the balcony gulping the rain-washed air. He was the least bit hungover from Anne Felton's scotch. He remembered her dispassionately. The kind of ruthless, headstrong woman who would always defeat her own desire to be needed. The sort of woman he'd have put into bed for the pale tan of her skin—the urgency of her voice in love— even the mockery that had crinkled her eyes. He'd 'phone her to-night, he decided. He could do a lot worse than Anne Felton. A guarded friendship with her would have no exigencies on either side. Each would be cynical of the other's intentions yet content to do nothing to disprove them. And God knows it would be a change to know a woman who could offer a little hospitality.

A crash from the balcony below meant that Colonel Buckley was adding another to the line of empty bottles he dumped on his balcony. Steel went inside. Strong black tea and cinder toast made a sketchy breakfast. When it was done, he made the choice of clothes with care. The occasion warranted it. Dark blue suit, white silk shirt, grey tie. He'd pick up a flower on his way to the Old Bailey.

He let the razor drone on his cheeks, shearing the blue stubble. Just twenty-four hours ago, the thought of Friday had been filled with foreboding. Christ! What a fool he'd felt that night in Felton's car. He was able to think of it now with amusement, the humiliation completely gone. There they'd all be at the Central Criminal Court—thousands of pounds of legal talent knocking itself out in a battle that *he* had already decided. Sheila— who would probably put Danny's discharge down to Divine intervention on her behalf. She had been hearing Mass every morning before going to the court. And Alan— ah well, the kid had done his best, more you couldn't do. Steel was in a generous mood yet taken with his own superiority. Suppose he told *nobody* about Felton. Let 'em all go on thinking how brilliant they'd been. It could be done! Alan was sure to stay buttoned-up. This fix hadn't cost Sullivan a nickel. Anne Felton wasn't an item to be entered into the car lot ledgers. Later perhaps, he might give Sullivan the whole story. He was one guy who would appreciate it.

Steel was whistling as he went down the stairs. Mrs. Kolmer opened her door just enough to show one eye and a drooping nose. "I took a telephone message for you yesterday afternoon," she said loftily. "A solicitor, the man said he was." Quite obviously she was delighted to pass on the news. She pulled the door a fraction towards her.

He waited, resisting the urge to trap her nose in the wood. "Well?" he said sourly.

"The message was that *that man's* trial's going to be

finished to-day. And - I - hope - he - gets - ten - years," she finished in a rush and slammed the door shut.

He went out to the street remembering that tomorrow he must find another place to live. It wouldn't be a bad idea to get out of Chelsea. Regent's Park appealed to him till he realized that it was because it was near Anne Felton. He wondered at the frequency with which he was thinking of the juryman's wife.

At nine o'clock in the morning, the King's Road was jammed with city-bound traffic. Steel used the back doubles and parked by the bus queue beyond the corner movie. Then he left the car and walked round to the quiet square. As he moved up to Felton's house, he was bouncing in spite of the aches. Having this certainty—this secret knowledge—was like being on a dog track and having five dogs in the bag. Sure that five of the runners were doped. All round, the suckers were shoving one another over to get to the bookmakers and the tote. Just to put good money on greyhounds that might as well have had three legs.

He suddenly remembered the dozen times when he himself had lost money on rigged races. Gone for some "Certainty" in a heat where one of the boys had a kennel maid fixed. Then *something* had gone wrong. Either the girl lost her nerve at the last minute, or the dog you wanted to win broke a leg, fell over or was left twenty lengths. These were the unpredictable things that made a certainty a joke unless you did the business yourself. There was only one way to fix a race or a jury—do it yourself. That's what he *had* done. Now, nothing could go wrong as long as he got Felton to the Central Criminal Court in one piece and talking sense.

He rang the juryman's doorbell. Inside, the radio newscast was loud. To-night, the guy would be reading the result of the trial with precisely the same inflection as he used for the Produce Market prices.

"The trial of Daniel Sullivan for attempted murder ended to-day at the Central Criminal Court when a jury was unable, for the second time, to reach a verdict. Sullivan's release was ordered by Justice Croxon."

The door opened. Felton was dressed ready for the street—his bruised eyes hidden behind dark glasses. The strip of plaster had been replaced with a small patch. Steel went into the hall and sat down without bothering to take off his coat. Felton leaned his broad back against the door. "Is this wise—coming here like this in broad daylight?" asked the juryman.

"Take off the glasses," Steel ordered. The swellings round the juror's eyes had gone down but the flesh remained an angry purple. His own hurts forgotten, Steel grinned. "Somebody's going to ask you how you got those——" he nodded, "—what are you going to tell them?"

Felton replaced the glasses, hiding his hate behind the dark lens. "That I walked into a door," he said sourly.

Steel shook his head and turned down his mouth. "You can do better than that, with your imagination!" The big guy was a bag of nerves—needed settling down. "Take it easy, Felton," said Steel. "You've got nothing to worry about. Forget these movies you write. There's no cop with a camera on my tail—nobody has the house wired. You're an honest citizen, my friend. Called to the highest duty an honest citizen can fulfill." He pulled the envelope from his pocket and read the address slowly.

"H.M. Inspector of Taxes—Charles House."

He tapped the paper. "Just as soon as I see Sullivan walk out of the dock, this gets torn up. If not—" he hunched his shoulders.

Felton went through to the drawing-room and cut the radio. When he came back, he asked Steel nervously:

180

"How sure are you about this second trial business. I mean, suppose the jury comes to a deadlock and then they put Sullivan on trial again. How do I stand?"

"You'll have done your part," Steel said quietly. "Let me worry about that. You get yourself a good lunch and be prepared to sit in the jury's room all night, if necessary. Act naturally. You're a man with a sincere belief in Sullivan's innocence. That's all there is to it."

Felton nodded. "That's all there is to it." He managed an unconvincing laugh. "I don't have any choice in what *I'm* doing."

"You sound as though you think I have," Steel countered. "Also as if you think I might welsh. You better remember this for the rest of your life, Felton. People on my side of the fence don't give their word lightly. If you're on the level, you'll never hear from me again. One thing—*nobody* knows about this except you and me."

Both men had the same thought and it showed on their faces. "And Anne," said Felton.

"And Anne," Steel agreed. "Only that's a headache that you acquired long before I came on the scene." He stood up and straightened his tie in the mirror. "What do you usually do with trouble, Felton?" He held up a hand stopping the other. "Don't tell me—it goes with the rest of the things they taught you at school." Steel made his voice sonorous. "You Face Up To It! Well, that's for the birds, friend. If you can't beat it, you run away from it. Your best bet with Anne is to put as many miles between the pair of you as possible." He put his hand out. "You can grab it," he said. "This isn't Dear Old Pals. It's a pledge that I'll do everything that I've said I would. Everything," he repeated significantly. Their hands gripped for a moment then Steel thumbed the catch on the street door. "Whichever way it goes, you won't see

me again—not socially. Be lucky!" He pulled the door
shut after him.

He made one stop on the way to the Old Bailey, to buy
a red carnation. It was still early and there was space in
front of the court building. He left the car and walked up
to the Post Office. In the booth, he found the number he
wanted. *La Speranza Restaurant*. The name couldn't have
been more appropriate and they served the best food west
of Knightsbridge. Steel booked a table for four. Let Galt
buy his own meal, he thought. There was only one drink
when a man came home from jail or beat a rap. He
ordered the champagne from a vintage year and in
magnums. Eight o'clock was a good hour. The verdict
would be through by then with luck—he had the feeling
that Croxon would not press an obviously divided jury
too far. When the voice the other end asked what name,
Steel grinned "Daniel Sullivan" he said. "And party."

Had he known that goddam flower language, he'd have
ordered a basketful of the appropriate flowers for Sheila.
Lack of Faith. By the time he reached the Old Bailey,
the hall upstairs was crowded. Steel recognized a half-
dozen cops from the Yard. For the most part from the
Heavy Mob—the Flying Squad. Bates was there and the
two who'd been with him in the Draycott Place raid the
other morning. The young cop who'd been so ready with
his hands stared Steel all the way up the stairs. Like
carrion crows, they were, Steel thought—ready to attend
the kill. Over against the 'phone booths, Galt's fat back
was wobbling as he used arms and shoulders in explanation of some point to Sheila and Alan. Steel went across
to them. They were as bad as the cops, he thought, looking
at their faces with impatience. All they needed was a
hearse. Their expressions were right for it.

His carnation was almost an affront to Sheila's severe
black coat. That nose-length veil probably hid red eyes.

Instead of using the hours, making herself prettier for Sullivan, she'd have been sitting up all night. As he put his cheek against hers, she averted it.

"Oh, for Crissakes stop acting like Mary Magdalene!" he burst out irritably. "What do you think this is, a wake?"

Alan broke in. "She didn't sleep too well, Gerry." Behind Sheila's back, he was making signals—jerking his head towards the steps. "Where's the loo?" he asked pointedly.

Short of spelling it out, thought Steel, the kid couldn't have made his concern more obvious. "I'll show you in a minute," he said. He whacked Galt's pin-striped shoulder a fraction harder than the gesture warranted. "Here we are!" he cracked. "The big day! I got your message. The grounded witch who runs my place had a lot of pleasure giving it to me. 'I-hope-he-gets-ten-years!' she shrieked and vanished with a strong smell of brimstone." Pleased with the picture, he smiled. No-one else did.

"I've got to have a couple of words with you, Gerry," said Galt. The razor had left his face shining. His small feet were in gleaming shoes. Not a crease showed in the broadcloth shirt. His suit was impeccable.

A real smooth article, thought Steel. Plump and prosperous on thieves' money yet discernibly patronizing to them. Just a few more hours and Galt would be tipping about on his toes, smiling that fat smile and waiting for praise if not gratitude. They were standing just out of earshot of Sheila and her brother.

"I've got a bit of bad news, Gerry," Galt said. Whatever the reason, his concern seemed real enough.

At that moment, Felton and a couple of jurors passed through the hall on the way to their room. *Nothing* could be bad news, Steel wanted to tell Galt. But he made his face long to match the other's. "Not more money?" he kidded.

Galt shook his head. "Sullivan's closing down," he said quietly. "Everything. He's selling the business, lock, stock and barrel. As from Monday, Sullivan Motors ceases to exist. I've been told to get all the papers from you. Bankbooks, stock sheets, the ledgers. I've made an appointment with the accountants for Monday morning."

Steel knew that the colour of his face must have changed. Ignoring the No Smoking sign, he lit a cigarette. "It's all news to me," he said slowly. "On whose instructions is all this being done?"

"Sullivan's," Galt answered. "I opened the letter an hour ago. It's dated yesterday and sent from the prison." Hand half-way to his breast pocket, he added, "Do you want to see it?"

Steel moved his hand through his thatch of hair. "Why should I want to see it?" he said bitterly. Sheila and Alan had moved farther up the hall. Though you couldn't tell which way her eyes were looking, behind that veil, he had the feeling she was watching. The certainty was strong that she had known what her husband had done, last night. It explained her strangeness on the 'phone. And that's how she's spent the half-hour they'd let her talk to Danny. Influencing him. Sure—working on him to wind up everything in England and pull out for Australia—South Africa. One of these countries where you were meant to Make Good. Some place where there would be a chance to live without Koskys and Yorks. And maybe without Steels! he thought suddenly. How would *he* fit into this mass emigration scheme! But Sullivan wasn't made that way, he told himself, some of the warm confidence returning. All right—maybe the business *was* to be wound up. Suppose Danny took Sheila and the kid and pulled out of this rat race. It wouldn't be without seeing that Steel had the chance to earn a crust.

One thing. If Sheila wasn't an enemy, she could hardly

be counted a friend. Remembering her averted cheek—her strangeness the night before—he knew that already Sheila had accepted the new status. He was no longer Gerry, reliable Brutus Steel. Just a link with Sullivan's past that Sheila wanted to chop adrift. Even that was all right. At least it put things in proper perspective. To-night, they'd be eating at the *Speranza*. When they'd eaten and drank their goddam champagne, he'd let them know just how Sullivan had been freed. If Sullivan wanted to put a cash value on it, fair enough. That seemed to be what their friendship had come to.

"O.K.," he told the lawyer. "I'll see you have everything by tomorrow morning." He couldn't resist the question. "What's gotten into him, Galt? He must have a reason for doing this!"

Galt's head was bent. He was rolling a match under the sole of his tiny foot. He looked up suddenly. "Remember something you said to me last week, Gerry? About doing what Sullivan told you? It's the same with me. I'm his lawyer. He gives me instructions not explanations."

They walked back to Sheila and her brother. Galt was busy with advice to Sheila about her evidence. He intended calling her for the defence. Steel watched her grave attentive mouth, her quiet manner, amazed that her naivete persisted. Did she *really* think this fat phoney was going to walk Danny out of the dock! Ah well. When the time came for her knowing the truth, there'd be a lot of comfort in her chagrin. Bitch a man's job completely and then find out that he saved your husband from ten years on the Moor. Whatever else, Sheila was too sincere—hell too *decent* was the word—not to feel sorry. And her sorrow she could poke in a pig's ear, he told himself.

Alan was still making laboured faces at Steel. The pair of them went down to the lavatories. Steel gave his coat to the attendant and went to the mirror, settling his flower to best advantage. The hell with 'em all. This was the last time he stuck his neck out for anyone except himself. He pulled the thin edge of linen a fraction higher from his breast pocket. Alan's nervousness was tiresome. Steel grinned encouragement. "You want to know what happened with Felton!" he jibed. "Well, I don't give up easily. The tougher the going, the better I like it, Alan." Boy—he thought secretly—what a line *that* turned out to be! "Danny's as good as on the street." He jerked his head. "C'mon. They'll be waiting."

Alan halted him. "There's something funny going on with Sheila. Ever since yesterday afternoon, she's been acting strangely. You know, Gerry," he said hesitantly. "We've always been pretty close, Sheila and I. Whenever there's been trouble, she's told me. Now, she's got nothing to say. If I ask what's the matter, she tells me nothing and goes off and buries herself with the kid. What do you make of it, Gerry?"

"It's what conscience does for you," Steel told Alan. "Sheila persuaded Danny to sell out—every stick—when she saw him in the cells yesterday afternoon. As from Monday, I have no job. I ought to have had my head examined," he said sarcastically. "All the signs were there. The Swiss Family Sullivans. You ought to go along on the trip and take the pictures, Alan." He laughed shortly. "Unless your sister's persuaded Sullivan to turn back his loot to the insurance companies as well. If he's as far gone as that, he belongs in a little white cot with curtains round it. We shouldn't be anywhere near him. Neither you *nor* me!" One hand in the small of the younger man's back, Steel propelled him through the door.

CHAPTER XII

ALL the way up the stairs, Steel was a couple of paces behind Alan. As they reached the main hall, a hand pulled Steel's arm. He whipped round like a nervous horse at the starting gate.

"Good morning, Gerry!" Anne Felton held him for a moment by the lapels of his coat. "Don't be frightened," she smiled. Her face was mocking but her voice kind. "I'm not going to kiss you. Not that I wouldn't like to—" she said softly. Nodding at Sheila, she asked: "You were talking to her just now. Who is she?"

He pulled her into the huddle of witnesses and forced a couple of seats free on the marble bench. "You must be out of your mind! What in hell have you come here for!" In this drab crowd, there'd be nobody who'd miss her elegance. Her long fair hair was topped with a tiny Juliet cap. She wore sapphire squares in her ears and a dark mink wrap. Her scent fogged some of his resentment. "A couple of minutes ago, your husband walked through there. And the place is crummy with cops. The woman you're talking about is Sullivan's wife." People on the bench beside them were turning their heads to look. "Suppose you'd pulled this trick when Felton walked through," Steel said savagely. "He says hello to you, you say hello to me, I say hello to Sullivan's wife. That's all the cops need to throw the lot of us into jail." He brought his hand down sharply on the marble bench. "You're fooling around with a man's liberty, Anne. Mine, too, if that means anything."

187

While he talked she watched the crowd of cops, lawyers and witnesses with interest. Now she smiled at Steel, shaking her head. "I'm not nearly as stupid as you seem to think, darling. I 'phoned Clive this morning. He knew I was coming here and I made sure that he wouldn't acknowledge me. Besides, I *wanted* to come." She slid her fingers inside his sleeve. "Don't I have the right?" she asked softly.

"The *right?*" He moved uneasily. "*What* right?" he started—faint lines showed between her eyes and he back-pedalled. "I guess it's all right, baby. As long as we're sure Felton isn't going to start waving to you or something, there's no harm done." He was uncertain what happened now.

From the other side of the hall, Galt and Alan had turned round, looking in the direction of the bench. Only Sheila still faced the other way.

"You must introduce me to your friends," Anne said calmly. Deliberately, she tucked her arm into his as they neared the other three.

Conscious of Sheila's appraisal behind the veil, Steel forced his voice to the right measure of ease. "May I introduce some friends of mine? This is Sheila Sullivan—Alan Prentiss—Felix Galt. This is Anne Curtis," he invented.

One quick look at the mink, the Delman shoes, the jewelled ears and Galt was his blandest. Alan stammered some sort of acknowledgment, recognition showing in his eyes. He turned them on the knot of detectives as if he expected to be arrested on the spot.

"If you're a friend of Gerry's thank you for coming," said Sheila. "Gerry's a good friend of my husband's too. Has he told you about my husband?" Her voice was low but there was no shame in it.

Anne's hand went out impulsively, touching Sheila's

sleeve. "Gerry's told me—I'm sure everything's going to be all right, Mrs. Sullivan."

"I know it is," Sheila was positive.

Steel tried for words to break the tension. He fumbled like an actor who's forgotten his lines. This false sentimentality sickened him. These two women ready to weep on one another's shoulders. And Galt with that bogus gallantry. Even Alan who looked ready to curl up and die. All were as far removed from the reality of Danny's plight as a pig from a palace. They'd do better to go sit in the car and emote while he watched Felton settle the issue.

"Come on," he said suddenly. "It's time we went into court."

The fat lawyer touched his bow-tie with inelegant fingers. "If I'd known you were coming, Mrs. Curtis . . ."

"Sure, you'd have baked a cake!" Steel interrupted. Under his baleful glare, the lawyer strutted away self-consciously.

The small party went into the court. That mink had its uses, thought Steel. One look at Anne and the cop at the door found them places by the side of the dock. Sheila was at the end of the row, a dozen feet from where her husband would sit. The dock was empty, the three chairs lined with precision. In front of Sullivan's, on the ledge, was a scratch pad and pencil.

The court was even fuller than it had been these past days. Steel looked up to see the cop in the Public Gallery closing the doors. Outside would be the notice.

COURT FULL

At the back of the benches usually reserved for witnesses, the Scotland Yard contingent crammed their thick bodies, one against the other. All waiting for Sullivan's conviction and sentence, Steel told himself. All ready to spread the news—this time, Sullivan's fixed for keeps.

He sneaked a look at Felton. If the juror *had* recognized his wife, he'd made no sign. A trifle sinister behind the dark lens, he sat straight in his seat, the model of intelligent appreciation. Steel almost nodded approval—like a film director pleased with his star's performance.

Under cover of the stir of the judge's arrival, Trelawney smiled some remark at Clarke who nodded. Each of the three seats on the judge's bench was occupied. Croxon in the centre. One by a judge in robes, the other by a be-ruffled civic dignitary. The Clerk of the Court read the jury roster monotonously. As if he, at least, were determined to stress that this was simply another day. Felton answered his name in a clear voice, adjusted his glasses and sat down. Anne Felton's fingers dug into Steel's arm.

Now the shuffling feet were still and the court was quiet. Here and there, a self-conscious sufferer stifled a cough or sneeze. For a few seconds, the tick of the clock on the wall was distinct. Judge Croxon nodded and the warder in the dock snapped his fingers at the man waiting below.

Sullivan was paler than he'd looked before. The scar on his neck angrier. As he saw Sheila, he stopped for a second. Then he moved his head as if saying something then sat down. His eyes were for nobody else. Sheila sat the way she had been when Sullivan came from below. Body half-turned towards the dock, a finger at her mouth. She watched as Sullivan took the scratch pad from in front of him and wrote. He folded the paper, signalling Galt. The fat lawyer bustled over and took the note. At the table, Galt read it, one hand shielding the contents from the eyes of York on the other side of the table. Then the lawyer passed it to Clarke with a whispered comment.

One hand on the back of the bench, Clarke leaned back. Not only his face but the whole position of his body expressed incredulity. He read the note again then got to his feet. He addressed Croxon. "I have just had a communication passed to me, m'lord, that makes it necessary for me to confer with the defendant."

Croxon leaned down, joining his hands. His voice was mild but firm. "You know, I can't adjourn for very long, Mr. Clarke. The jury has been very patient in this case and I'm anxious to finish to-day, if possible."

"An adjournment won't be necessary, m'lord. I can talk to him here."

Croxon nodded assent. Sullivan leaned from the dock, talking into Clarke's ear. The accused man shook his head adamantly in reply to the lawyer's response. Shrugging, Clarke went back to his seat. As he passed Galt, Clarke said something.

Steel's eyes were on Sheila. Her lips were moving but without sound. The glove in her fingers was twisted to a tangled piece of skin. Like an animal that senses danger, Steel's head swung towards Felton. The juryman hadn't changed position but sat, inscrutable, his eyes hidden.

Clarke rose to his feet a little wearily. "I shall have to ask the Court's indulgence, m'lord. I have just received instructions to enter a plea of guilty to the indictment." He sat down and covered the papers in front of him with his brief case.

For Steel, that first moment, it was as if someone had half-bludgeoned him from behind. He swung in angry disbelief. Sheila still had her face turned to Sullivan in the dock. Her cheeks were wet but unheeded. *Now* Steel remembered her voice in the churchyard. Insistent with her crazy ideas of right and wrong. He had paid no attention to the lunatic approach to reality, he recalled. And this is how it had turned out! Ever since that day— before, maybe—Sheila must have been working on Sullivan to plead guilty. Surrendering her husband's

191

liberty for the screwball ideals that she'd brought from the backwoods. Friend! She was no more than a treacherous little tramp.

Unconsciously, he was leaning forward, glaring at her and half out of his seat. Anne caught the back of his coat, pulling him down on the bench. "I can't believe it—Sullivan's gone crazy." His voice was loud enough to turn the heads of a couple of men sitting in front. As they turned, Anne shushed Steel to silence. For a second, Steel thought of passing a note to Galt—to Clarke—*anybody*. And what did you say *Take back that plea! I've bribed one of the jury!* Surely, there *had* to be a way out. Some way of stopping this insanity! "I've got to do *something!*" He said again. Frowning, Anne shook her head.

Croxon's voice was clear as he peered over his glasses. "If the person responsible for that disturbance is not quiet, he will be removed from this court!"

Steel put his hands over his ears and stared at the floor between his legs, trying to block out all sound. But Croxon's voice persisted. "You understand the implications of this plea, do you, Sullivan?" he asked.

Sullivan stood, a very tired-looking man. "Yes, my lord."

Heads were craning from the Public Gallery and in the jury box Felton turned in his seat. In spite of the dark glasses, he faced the body of the court with obvious bewilderment.

"Very well," said Croxon. He bent over and whispered to the Clerk of the Court. "Mr. Clarke?" he invited.

Clarke rose. "I understand that the prisoner's wife is in court, m'lord. I would like to call her." As fat as the other was thin, Galt rose in turn. Both lawyers watched as Sheila walked to the box slowly and took the oath.

Clarke's voice was deep with sympathy. "Your name is Sheila Sullivan, married woman, and wife of the prisoner?"

192

She turned her head so that she faced the dock. Then she lifted her veil. "I am proud to be his wife," she said quietly. As Clarke drew the questions from her, one after another, the faces in court watching her relaxed with understanding. Clarke leaned towards her, both hands on the wood in front of him. "I am sure everyone in this court must have a great deal of sympathy for you, Mrs. Sullivan. You have told us that as a husband and father, the prisoner's conduct has been exemplary. I have just one more question—should this court take a lenient course, would you be willing to return to your husband?"

"There's no question of that," she answered. "I have never left him nor he me. When I married Danny, he made me a promise that he kept till this happened. He's going to pay dearly for it." She shook her head. "I'm not his judge, Mr. Clarke. I'm his wife. No matter *what* happens to him, I shall still be his wife."

Trelawney waived cross-examination. As Sheila walked to the back of the court, she passed Steel without a look. She moved with a high head but wet cheeks. Alan slipped from the bench and joined his sister.

Clarke ignored the jury now, his voice still pitched low. "M'lord, I have specific instructions from the prisoner to make no plea in mitigation. He acknowledges his guilt and is ready to accept the consequence. But in spite of this instruction, m'lord, there are two things that I feel duty-bound to mention. Sullivan is charged under the Criminal Justice's Act of 1948 as a person liable for Corrective Training or Preventive Detention as an Habitual Criminal. M'lord, there can be no question but that Sullivan has the statutory qualifications. He has been convicted eight times for felonies in this country. Twice the amount necessary for the purposes of the Act. The report of the Prison Commissioners suggests that Sullivan is not suitable for Corrective Training but suitable for Preventive Detention. We know what that means, m'lord. Ten or twelve years with the damned—the hopeless for companions. I suggest, with the greatest respect, that now, if ever, is the time to give Sullivan the opportunity to redeem himself that has always been denied him. Time after time, this man has been sent to jail; never has any judge seen fit to extend leniency to him. The other matter I speak of is related, m'lord. No-one who heard this man's wife speak on his behalf could fail to appreciate her honesty—decency. It has been because of Sullivan's knowledge of her high principles and his strong regard for her that he now pleads guilty. Could *any* man have a better companion than this in an attempt at rehabilitation!" Clarke gathered a couple of papers before him and finished, "I am confident your lordship will pass such sentence as will be an encouragement to all men such as this who wish to put the past behind them." He sat down.

Croxon's head was bent as he listened to York's evidence of antecedents. The broken-toothed detective read from the Criminal Record Office folder with pleasure. "The prisoner is forty-five, sir. And a native of London. His first conviction goes back to . . ." a heavy thumb flipped back a couple of sheets in the dossier. ". . . 1919, sir. He was then sentenced to the care of the Saint Vincent de Paul Society as a truant and person beyond control of his lawful guardians." York cleared his throat. Next, sir— m'lord . . ." The dreary litany of years spent behind walls droned on. Croxon broke in impatiently, lifting his long head with decision. "That's enough—that's enough," he said irritably. "We don't want to hear all that, officer. I'm very much against these long-winded recitals of every detail of a prisoner's antecedents. Just give the man's last conviction and leave it at that."

194

Rebuffed, York gave the date and sentence, closed the dossier and went back to the solicitor's table.

For a moment, Croxon sat with his head down. The high-back chair seemingly too large for him. Then, folding his hands, he sat erect. Monotonously but clearly, the clock on the wall recorded the passing seconds. There were no shuffling feet—no stifled cough—to detract from the dispassionate voice.

"Sullivan, you have pleaded guilty to attempted murder. You told me—as did your eminent counsel—that you fully understand the implications of this plea. Indeed, they are plain. Yours was an attempt to kill Edward Kosky by shooting at him with a pistol. Violence of any kind has always been foreign to the people of this country. It is an aversion our forefathers translated into laws for the protection of everyone within the scope of their jurisdiction. Not only those who live their lives in exemplary fashion— no less than anyone else, the self-confessed murderer is himself protected from violence. We pride ourselves in England that no man shall go in fear of his life without the protection of the law.

"Throughout the course of this trial, both sides have made much of matters extraneous to the real issue. I want you to realize this, Sullivan. You have pleaded guilty to one crime and one crime only here this day. It is solely for this offence that you will be sentenced." The old voice was firm as if anxious to stress some inner belief that was strong. "There appears to be a widespread belief in certain quarters that a criminal is punished twice. Once for the offence that he has committed and secondly for previous but purged offences. In this court, at least, that is false. Although a man's previous criminal history is considered, as is any other evidence as to character, of itself it carries no indefinite penalty. You have not seen fit to plead provocation. Yet from such evidence as we

195

have heard, some degree of provocation seems likely. Other than saying that *nothing* justifies the use of violence I have no wish to comment on the personalities of certain witnesses for the Crown. We are used to hearing a great deal from learned counsel about the desirability of clemency. It is true that to-day, a child—a youth—would be treated with greater leniency than you have been in the past. In your case, it is debatable whether leniency would have changed the course of your life. I have been greatly impressed by the sincerity of your wife. It may well be that, through her, lies your salvation. Solely because of this belief, I am not going to sentence you as an habitual criminal. You will go to prison for five years."

For the first time, Steel brought himself to look up at the dock. Facing the judge, Sullivan nodded slightly and wiped the back of his hand across his mouth. The Code, Steel remembered, required a faint smile of defiance yet Sullivan showed only relief. The prisoner's hoarse voice croaked. "Thank you, sir." Between two jailers, he went down the steps to the cells.

Croxon beckoned York. "Officer. You will see that arrangements are made for this man's wife to see him before he is taken to prison." Dwarfed by the Under-Sheriff, the judge walked slowly through the door to his chambers.

With the tension gone, there was a loud babble as people crowded into the aisles. After one last look at the public benches, Felton followed the other jurymen. York and his fellow-detectives passed the end of Steel's aisle. The cop made his voice a snarl just loud enough to register—"The old fool's getting soft." As Steel looked up, York gave a gaped grin. "If you're looking for a job, Gerry, I'll give you a reference. Willing but stupid!"

It seemed a long time before Anne touched his arm. Steel moved his head uncertainly. The cop who had been on the door was leaning over the bench. "We're closing the court now, sir." Under Steel's blank stare the man moved ponderously up the aisle to straighten a chair at the empty table.

An old man in carpet slippers was sweeping round the bare stone benches. Anne held Steel's arm tightly, the sound of her heels echoing in the high-ceilinged lobby. Downstairs, the last stragglers from the courtroom stood irresolute before the rain that fell in the street. At the end of the passage leading to the jailer's office, Sheila waited with Alan. Impulsively, Steel shook his arm free and went across the hall. Long before he reached them, Sheila and her brother had turned their heads, their faces dim in the shadows.

Now that he was close to her, Steel found no words. Only his eyes showed the sickness he felt.

"I had to do it, Gerry." Sheila put out a hand to touch his sleeve. Her face troubled, she repeated, "Gerry!" but he moved aside.

The boy came closer to his sister. "Don't take it out on her," he said quickly. "She knows all you tried to do for Danny. I told her."

Sheila's face was wet in the pale yellow light. "And you hate me for it," she said, shaking her head with certainty. "Danny couldn't go on running from trouble. Nobody can. Don't you see that, Gerry?" Her face was compassionate.

Bitterness released the words in his head and he gave them force. "I'll tell you what I see," he said slowly, wetting his mouth. "Nothing more than a goddamned hypocrite who's just sent her husband to jail for five years." The uniformed jailer was making his way towards them down the sombre passageway. "Give Danny my regards," Steel said deliberately. "And tell him *I'll* pray for him too. He's going to need it." He turned his back and walked a thousand miles to where Anne took both his hands in hers.

"Stop it, Gerry," she said swiftly. "There's nothing more you can do. Anyone can do. It was Sullivan's choice and you did your best." She touched the flower in his lapel. "You should be thinking about celebrating." Her voice was almost arch. "There's nothing that can keep us apart, now."

He nodded, suddenly tired. There were so many things to be done. Prepare all the papers for Galt. Cancel that table at the *Speranza*. Find a new place to live.

He fumbled for his car keys and an envelope fell to the floor.

H.M. Inspector of Taxes
Charles House

He tore it to shreds and held them in his hand.

Anne pulled the mink firmly round her. "Well, for God's sake don't look so desperate," she said drily. "It isn't *you* who've been sent to jail!"

He gripped the torn envelope in his pocket as if it were some talisman and followed her out to the wet street.

>>> If you've enjoyed this book and would like to discover more great vintage crime and thriller titles, as well as the most exciting crime and thriller authors writing today, visit: >>>

The Murder Room
Where Criminal Minds Meet

themurderroom.com